Lovingly
Alice

Books by Phyllis Reynolds Naylor

Witch's Sister
Witch Water
The Witch Herself
Walking Through the Dark
How I Came to Be a Writer
How Lazy Can You Get?
Eddie, Incorporated
All Because I'm Older
Shadows on the Wall
Faces in the Water
Footprints at the Window
The Boy with the Helium Head
A String of Chances
The Solomon System
Bernie Magruder and the Case of the Big Stink
Night Cry
Old Sadie and the Christmas Bear
The Dark of the Tunnel
The Agony of Alice
The Keeper
Bernie Magruder and the Disappearing Bodies
The Year of the Gopher
Beetles, Lightly Toasted
Maudie in the Middle
One of the Third Grade Thonkers
Alice in Rapture, Sort Of
Keeping a Christmas Secret
Bernie Magruder and the Haunted Hotel
Send No Blessings
Reluctantly Alice
King of the Playground
Shiloh
All but Alice

Lovingly Alice

Phyllis Reynolds Naylor

Atheneum Books for Young Readers

NEW YORK · LONDON · TORONTO · SYDNEY

Atheneum Books for Young Readers
An imprint of Simon & Schuster Children's Publishing Division
1230 Avenue of the Americas, New York, New York 10020

Book design by Ann Sullivan
The text for this book is set in Berkeley Oldstyle.
Manufactured in the United States of America
First Edition
2 4 6 8 10 9 7 5 3 1
Library of Congress Cataloging-in-Publication Data
Naylor, Phyllis Reynolds.
Lovingly Alice / Phyllis Reynolds Naylor.—1st ed.
p. cm.
Summary: Fifth grade is tumultuous for Alice as she tries to help others
through the many changes occurring at home and in school, including
learning about sex when Rosalind gets her period and shares a book that
explains what is happening.
ISBN 0-689-84399-2
[1. Friendship—Fiction. 2. Single-parent families—Fiction. 3. Family
life—Fiction. 4. Schools—Fiction. 5. Menstruation—Fiction. 6. Sex—
Fiction. 7. Maryland—Fiction.] I. Title.
PZ7.N24Lo 2004   [Fic]—dc22
2003023504

To Grace Isabelle Murphy Meis,
lovingly

Contents

1

Gone

My dad says there are good years and bad years for wine. I think there are good years and bad years for kids, too. My fifth-grade year in particular.

I'll admit I started out as sort of a grump, first because my brother celebrated his eighteenth birthday and asked for lemon cake, which I hate.

"Why don't you really go for it, Lester, and ask for prune cake?" I said. "Crab apple cake with grapefruit frosting?"

"Nobody's making you eat it, Al," he told me. My full name is Alice Kathleen McKinley, but Dad and Lester call me Al.

The second thing that made me grumpy was that I ripped a pocket on my favorite jeans, and it was hanging by one seam.

My mother died when I was in kindergarten, and Dad can't sew very well. He can cook and clean, but it takes him a long time to sew on a button or something. I don't know how to sew either so I have to walk around with a flapping pocket.

And the third thing that happened was that one of my very best friends, Sara, moved away. Rosalind, my other best friend, was as surprised as I was.

"Did *you* know she was going to move?" I asked Rosalind.

Rosalind shook her head. "Maybe she didn't know either. Maybe she just woke up one morning and her dad said, 'Let's move.'"

We were sitting on the school steps waiting for the bell. It was as though one minute Sara was here, and the next she wasn't. There were other girls we hung around with at school, but we didn't like them as much as we'd liked Sara.

Megan was okay, even though she has a bratty little sister. Jody was sometimes okay and sometimes not. Dawn just did whatever Jody did.

"Bummer!" said Rosalind. "Sara was a lot of fun."

We watched Jody and Dawn staggering around the playground with their arms around each other's shoulders. They were pretending that Jody's right leg was tied to Dawn's left one, and they ended up giggling on the ground.

"We didn't know how much we'd miss Sara until she was gone," I said. Just like I didn't know how much I'd miss my mother until after she died, I guess. I should have enjoyed Sara as much as I could while she was still around. I decided to concentrate on Rosalind. She could make me laugh as much as Sara.

"Say something funny," I told her.

Rosalind wrinkled up her nose. "You can't just tell someone to be funny," she said. "It's only funny when you're not expecting it."

"Okay, I'll think about something else, and when I'm not expecting it, make me laugh," I said.

We were quiet for a moment.

"Donald Sheavers pulls snot," said Rosalind.

"What?" I cried. "Rosalind, that's not funny, it's gross!"

But she went right on. "You know how it is when you're getting over a cold and the snot gets thick as glue?"

"Rosalind!" I said again.

She wouldn't quit. "I saw him blowing his nose once, and every time he tried to grab the snot, it snapped back in like a rubber band."

"Euuuw!" I said.

Megan came up the walk just then. Everything about Rosalind is round, and everything about Megan is square. She dropped her backpack on the steps and sat down beside us.

"What were you talking about?" she asked.

"Snot," I said, and grinned.

"Oh!" said Megan, covering her ears.

"The rubber band kind that snaps back up your nostrils when you try to pull it out," said Rosalind.

"Stop it!" said Megan.

I laughed. "You did it," I said to Rosalind. "You made me laugh."

"You're welcome," said Rosalind.

When I walked home that afternoon with Donald Sheavers, I tried not to look at him. All I could think about was Donald having a cold. Donald blowing his nose.

We live next door to the Sheaverses, and Donald's mom used to take care of me on Tuesdays and Thursdays, but I don't have to go there anymore. And Lester doesn't have to come straight home from high school on Mondays, Wednesdays, and Fridays either, to look after me. The good thing about being in fifth grade is that I'm finally old enough to stay at home by myself.

"Cat got your tongue?" Donald asked me as we turned the corner onto our street.

"I miss Sara," I said. "I didn't know they were going to move."

"They got kicked out of their house because they

didn't pay their rent," Donald said. "If they hadn't moved quick, the sheriff would have put all their stuff out on the sidewalk."

I stopped dead still. "How do you know?"

"Mom heard some women talking about it at the beauty shop," he said.

Mrs. Sheavers works part-time at a hair salon, so she hears all kinds of stuff. But I sure didn't want to hear this.

"That's a lie, Donald," I said. "They wouldn't stop paying their rent."

"If they didn't have any money, they would," said Donald.

"But where would they go? If they don't have any money, where will they live?"

Donald shrugged. "In a tent, probably. Or maybe they just sleep in their car."

When Dad came home, I helped him make dinner. I stirred the tomato sauce while he boiled the spaghetti. My dad looks like a big teddy bear. He has thick hair at the sides of his head, not so much on top. It's a little gray above the ears, and the skin at the corners of his eyes crinkles when he smiles.

He was humming to himself as we cooked, but I was thinking about Sara. There were a lot of kids in her family. I tried to imagine them all living in a tent. Living in a *car*! I tried to imagine *us* living in *our* car. Dad sleeping on the front seat, maybe, and Lester stretched out in back.

When Lester got home and we finally sat down at the table, I said, "Dad, would you ever just wake me up some morning and say, 'Alice, let's move'?"

Dad paused with a forkful of spaghetti halfway to his mouth.

"Not unless he'd just robbed a bank or something," said Lester.

I toyed with my salad, turning a pickled beet over and over. "If we ever got so poor we had to live in our car, would I have to sleep on the floor?" I asked.

"Naw, we'd probably stick you under the hood, Al. Stuff you down between the engine and the radiator," said Lester.

"So who's moving and who's poor?" asked Dad.

"Sara," I said. "They had to leave because they couldn't pay their rent. Donald thinks maybe they're living in a tent or even their car."

"Well, I hope not!" said Dad. "There are places they can go for help, though." .

But why hadn't Sara asked *me* for help? I wondered. I would have given her all my money. I would have even gone around and collected money from neighbors, just so Sara could keep coming to our school.

* * *

I lay in bed that night thinking about her. About the way at first nobody liked the skinny girl who chewed with her mouth open and never washed her hair.

Then Rosalind and I invited her for a sleepover at my house, and we called it a shampoo party. We all washed our hair and brushed Sara's to show her how great it looked when it was clean, and we pretended we were rich ladies having tea at the Plaza, chewing our dainty sandwiches with our lips closed.

I wanted her back so I could tell her how funny she was, how smart she was, how many times she had made me laugh. Like the time I took a picture of her with coat hangers draped over her ears. And then she put two big buttons over her eyes and scrunched up her face to hold them there. I wanted her to know I loved her stories. Sara made up the scariest stories! Especially the one about a girl's mother who turns into a praying mantis and her arms drop off and she gets this long bony face with huge eyes and jaws! I wanted to tell her how much fun I'd had at her house once, playing in big boxes out in the yard and helping myself to whatever I wanted in the refrigerator for lunch.

Maybe Rosalind and I could go looking for her. If she was in a tent, maybe we'd find it. If she was sleeping in her family's car, maybe we'd see her there. I felt my mattress jiggle as Oatmeal, my gray and white cat, jumped up on my bed to sleep with me. I reached out and scratched her behind the ears in the darkness. She licked my hand, but she didn't purr. I didn't feel like purring either.

※ ※   2   ※ ※

Looking for Sara

I wanted to look for Sara, but I didn't want to go alone. I didn't want to tell Jody and Dawn and Megan either, because they were some of the girls who never liked her much. I was sure that if I told Jody that Sara's family got kicked out, she'd say, *It figures*.

At recess, when all *three* girls were pretending their legs were tied together, I told Rosalind to come back behind the building, and then I said, "I've got a secret, but you have to cross your heart and hope to die if you tell."

"I'll cross my heart, but I won't hope to die," said Rosalind. "But I won't tell, either."

"Okay," I said. "Donald Sheavers's mom heard that Sara's family got kicked out of their house because they couldn't pay the rent. He said they might be living in a tent or their car."

When Rosalind hears something interesting, her eyes open as wide and round as her face. She's sort of a large girl, and so is her stepmother. She has two older brothers and a dad, too. I could tell that she was trying to imagine her own family living in a car.

"Gosh. How embarrassing!" Rosalind said.

"No wonder she didn't tell us she was leaving," I said.

"So what do you think we should do?" Rosalind asked. That's what I like about Rosalind. She's always ready to *do* something.

"We could go look for her," I said.

"Then what?" she asked.

I guess I hadn't thought very much about "then what."

"I'd give her all my money," I said.

"It still wouldn't be enough to pay the rent," said Rosalind. "You'd have to sell something."

"Like what?"

"Like anything in your house that people would pay a lot of money for," said Rosalind.

I thought of each room in our house and tried to remember exactly what was in it. We're not very rich, so I wasn't sure what would sell for a lot of money. In fact, we're not rich at all. The biggest things in our house are the couch, the refrigerator, and Dad's bed, and I knew I'd better not try to sell those.

When I got home from school that day, I said, "Lester, do we have anything in this house that's worth a lot of money?" I wouldn't try to sell anything unless Dad said I could, of course, but I was just curious.

"My CD collection, maybe," said Lester. "Or my bike." He was sitting by the phone, waiting for a call from his girlfriend.

There are two girls who call Lester a lot—Lisa, his girlfriend, and Mickey, who would *like* to be his girl-friend. If Lisa liked Lester as much as he likes her, Lester would be really, really happy. If Lester liked Mickey as much as she likes him, *Mickey* would be really, really happy. The trouble with love is that it's not always the same people who love each other.

"So how much would you get for your CD collection if you sold it?" I asked.

"I'm not selling," said Lester.

The only thing I had a lot of were books. "If I sold all my books, how much would I get?" I asked him.

"Fifty cents a book, maybe. Why? What are you try-ing to do, anyway?" said Lester.

"Pay somebody's rent," I told him.

"You're nuts," said Lester.

The phone rang just then. Lester picked it up and took it into the coat closet, closing the door behind him.

If Rosalind and I found out that Sara's family was

living in a tent, I'll bet he'd sell his CD collection then.
If we found out they were living in a *car*, maybe Dad
would sell our *sofa*. When Saturday came, I was going
to ask Rosalind to walk around the neighborhood with
me and look for Sara.

My brother works part-time at a miniature golf course
on Saturdays. Dad is manager of a music store, the
Melody Inn, so he's gone on Saturdays too. I'm supposed to let Dad know where I'm going if I leave the
house, so I called the Melody Inn and left a message
with Loretta, the girl who runs the Gift Shoppe, a
place under the stairs where you can buy musical gifts.

"Please tell him I'm going to be out with Rosalind,"
I said.

"Gotcha," said Loretta.

When Rosalind came, she looked like she was going
on a safari. She was wearing a hat, sunglasses, and
binoculars on a strap around her neck, and she had a
backpack full of sodas and cheese crackers.

Rosalind is only a few months older than I am, but
she looks more grown up. She has two little bumps in
front under her T-shirt, only we don't talk about those.

"So where do you want to look?" Rosalind said.

"I guess we should look for a tent or a parked car
with a lot of people in it," I said.

"It's ten thirty on a Saturday morning," said Rosalind.

"If they're living in a car, they're not going to stay in there all day."

"Where would they go?" I wondered.

Rosalind shrugged. "They'd probably be standing on street corners begging for money, I guess."

I didn't like to think of Sara begging for money on street corners, and I wanted more than ever to find her. So we set out for the first place we could think of where someone might set up a tent—an empty lot over near the train tracks.

The lot was full of weeds. There was nothing in it but some empty Pepsi cans and an old tire.

"Where do we look next?" asked Rosalind.

"I'm thinking," I told her.

"Let's go sit down somewhere," said Rosalind. We walked over to a low wall by an automobile parts store, and Rosalind took off her backpack. She handed a can of Sprite to me and opened one for herself. Then she opened a package of cheese crackers.

We tried to think of all the other places we knew where someone could put up a tent.

"What about that lot behind the furniture store next to the alley?" I said. So we finished the Sprite and set out for the furniture store. I remembered the alley from the times we had driven by. I think I had seen some homeless people living there.

We walked seven blocks to the furniture store, and

when we went around to the alley, I knew right away that we shouldn't be there. A large cardboard box rested against a chain-link fence, with a man's jacket thrown over the top. An old chair sat beside the box. On down the alley, someone was in a sleeping bag, and farther still, there was a little shack made of tin and cardboard.

I looked at Rosalind and Rosalind looked at me. Then she looked at the shack through her binoculars.

"Do you see anybody?" I asked.

"No, but I see some feet sticking out," she said.

"Do you think it's Sara's family?"

"I don't know, and I'm not going down there to find out," she answered.

We decided to stay where we were at the end of the alley and just call out her name.

"One . . . two . . . three," I said, and then we both called together: "Sa-ra! Sa-ra!" We waited and called again. "Sa-ra!"

The sleeping bag began to move, and a man raised up and looked at us. "Shut up!" he yelled. "Get out of here."

But another man crawled out from the tin and cardboard shack.

"Who you want?" he called.

"Sara," we said.

"She's in here, darlin'. Come and look in here," he said.

Rosalind and I ran away as fast as we could. We didn't stop till we reached the corner. Rosalind opened another Sprite while we caught our breath.

"We shouldn't have gone back there," I said, feeling foolish. "We don't even know if they're still in town."

"We don't even know if they're in Maryland!" said Rosalind.

We headed back toward our neighborhood, peeking in parked cars as we went along to see if any looked as though a family had been sleeping inside. Then we stopped at the playground and swung awhile. When we finally got back to the house, Rosalind finished all her cheese crackers. We had been gone a long time. Maybe a couple of hours.

The phone rang. It was Dad.

"Alice, where have you been?" he asked. He sounded worried and angry both.

"Out with Rosalind," I said.

"That's not good enough," he said. "When you leave a message, I want to know exactly where you're going. I don't want you just wandering around. How would I know where to look if you didn't come home?"

"I'm sorry," I said.

"So where were you?" he asked.

"Looking for Sara," I said, in a small voice. "Donald Sheavers said she was probably living in a tent or a car."

There was silence at the other end of the line. Then Dad said, "Alice, are you there alone?"

"No, Rosalind's here," I said.

"Every time that girl comes over, there's trouble!" said Dad.

"It was *my* idea!" I told him. I didn't want him to tell me I couldn't see Rosalind. I didn't want to lose her, too.

"Okay, but I don't want you to leave the house. You and I are going to have a little talk when I get home," he said.

After he hung up, Rosalind asked, "What did he say?"

"That we're going to have a little talk when he gets home," I answered.

Rosalind picked up her backpack and put her hat on her head. "Gotta go," she said. "Bye."

I went over and sat down in my beanbag chair, waiting for Dad. If *this* was the way my fifth-grade year was going to go, I wondered, what was next?

3

Talking with Dad

I stayed in my room till suppertime. I thought that once Lester got home, Dad would forget about me. But he didn't.

"Where exactly did you and Rosalind go this afternoon when you were looking for Sara?" he asked as he helped himself to the turnips.

I swallowed. "That lot over by the tracks," I said, looking down at my plate.

"The railroad tracks? Alice, you *know* you're not supposed to go there!"

"We didn't get near them. We just looked at the empty lot," I said. And then, because Dad and Lester were staring at me, I added, "In case Sara's family was living in a tent."

Dad let out his breath. "Where else did you look?"

"The alley behind the furniture store," I whispered.

Dad dropped his fork. "You went down that alley?"

"No, we just stood at one end and called for Sara," I said.

"Good grief!" said Dad.

"Be glad she didn't try to sell our furniture," said Lester.

"*What?*" said Dad.

"She asked me what we could sell that would bring in some money," Lester told him. I gave him a look.

"Alice, what got into you?" Dad said. Now he just sounded tired. Really tired. "Maybe it's a mistake to let you stay here by yourself."

"No, Dad!" I cried. I couldn't stand the thought of having to go to the Sheaverses' again so that Donald's mom could look after me. And I knew that Lester would be mad if *he* had to stick around to make sure I didn't get into trouble. "I won't do it again!" I promised. "I just wanted to find her if she was living in a tent or a car."

"So you went around peeking in cars, too?" Dad asked.

"Just a few," I told him.

Dad shook his head. "Alice, what am I going to *do* with you?"

"You could always send her to a convent," said Lester, stabbing at his meat loaf.

"What's a convent?" I asked.

"A place where you pray all day long," said Lester.

That sounded almost worse than the Sheaverses'. And we were having meat loaf and turnips, which made the whole evening awful.

Dad gave a long sigh. "It was nice of you to think of Sara, sweetheart, but let's go over the rules again. If you don't think you can follow them, let me know. Number one: When you leave this house, I want you to call and tell me *exactly* where you're going. Got it?"

"Yes," I said.

"You're not to use the stove or the oven. You can put things in the microwave, but that's all."

"Right!" I said.

"You can have a few girls over, but no boys."

"No problem there," I told him.

"Never open the door to strangers."

I nodded.

"And you can make my bed, empty my wastebasket, and wash my socks," said Lester.

"Go jump," I said.

I thought "the talk" was over then, but Dad said, "And about Rosalind . . ."

"It wasn't her fault!" I cried. "Nothing was her fault! I asked her to go with me to look for Sara, and she did."

"Well, I wish you had at least one friend who would

open her mouth occasionally and say, 'No, Alice. We'd better not,'" said Dad.

When Rosalind called me later to find out what happened, I said, "Say, 'No, Alice, we'd better not.'"

"No, Alice, we'd better not," Rosalind repeated.

"Good. Now I'll tell Dad you said it," I told her.

Our teacher is Mrs. Swick, only we call her Mrs. Stick. She's young and as tall and straight and thin as a pencil. Her body looks stretched, like a Barbie doll's neck. The thing about Mrs. Swick is, she's not mean or anything, but she never laughs. On the playground the first week of school Donald Sheavers said that each of us should give a dime to the first person in our class who could make Mrs. Swick laugh out loud.

The second week of September, Jody dropped her carton of orange drink in the all-purpose room and it absolutely exploded. There was orange drink all over Jody. It even dripped from her nose. Everyone laughed, but Mrs. Swick didn't even smile.

The third week of September, Donald was reading a story from our literature book and he said the wrong word. He was supposed to read, "The artist slipped a little gold dust into his paints," but Donald said, ". . . into his pants." Everybody laughed except Mrs. Swick. She smiled, though.

The fourth week of September, on a really warm day, we had the windows open at the top and bottom both. A bird flew in and couldn't find its way out again. It kept flying around the room, swooping this way and that, and some of us were holding notebooks over our heads so the bird wouldn't poop on us. That made us laugh, but Mrs. Swick acted as though she couldn't take *one more thing*. The custodian came in and shooed the bird out.

When I told Lester about Mrs. Swick, he said that was a shame, because the most attractive thing about a girl is her laugh. If you can make a girl laugh, it means she likes you. I met Mickey once, the girl who likes Lester more than he likes her, and *she* laughs a lot.

"Can you make Mickey laugh whenever you want?" I asked him.

"The problem with Mickey is, she never stops," said Lester.

"Make up your mind," I told him.

But that's what I'd liked about Sara. She laughed a lot too. Even though her hair was too stinky sometimes and even though some of the other girls were mean to her and even though her family didn't have a lot of money, she could make us all laugh. Rosalind makes me laugh too, but not as much as Sara.

* * *

"Les," Dad said to him one evening in October, "I want you to be here Friday night. I'm going to a concert at the Kennedy Center."

"Oh, jeez, Dad! I wanted to go somewhere with Lisa!" said Lester.

"Well, please make it another night, because someone gave me two tickets for the National Symphony, and I've invited a friend."

Lester and I looked at each other.

"Male or female?" asked Lester.

"It happens to be a woman," said Dad.

I remembered that a customer had given Dad some chocolates on Valentine's Day. "Is it the same person who gave you the valentine candy?" I asked.

"No, not Elaine," said Dad, laughing. "She doesn't believe in candy. That was someone else."

"Aha!" said Lester.

"What? Aren't I allowed to have friends?" said Dad.

"Just curious," said Lester. "So there are two women chasing you!"

"Not exactly," said Dad.

On Friday night I watched Dad get ready from my room across the hall. Lester has a bed in the basement, but Dad has one of our bedrooms and I have the other one.

Dad put on a shirt with French cuffs. Then he put

on gold cuff links. He chose a blue tie with little white dots on it. He polished his shoes and trimmed his fingernails, and when he was done, he squirted on some cologne.

I went to the door of his room and studied him as he ran a cloth over his shoes to make them shine.

"What's Elaine like?" I asked. I wasn't too sure about a woman who didn't believe in candy.

"She's very nice," said Dad.

"What does she look like?"

"Well, she's not too tall, not too short, not too fat, not too thin, not too loud, not too soft, not too—"

"Dad!" I said.

He smiled. "She's just a woman I like a lot."

It was the "a lot" that made me perk up my ears. "Are you going to marry her?" I asked.

"Sweetheart, we haven't got that far," he said.

Lester and I fixed macaroni and cheese to eat while Dad went to dinner with Elaine what's-her-name. He wouldn't tell us her last name because she had children in school, he said, and if we knew who they were, it might make things awkward.

"*I* think it would be awkward if we told a friend our dad was dating this fox named Elaine, and it turned out that Elaine was this friend's mother," said Lester.

"Then I suggest you don't tell any of your friends that I'm dating a fox named Elaine," said Dad.

"If she has children, what happened to her husband?" I asked.

"They're divorced," said Dad.

Lester stayed in the basement most of the evening listening to CDs and playing his guitar. When the phone rang, he didn't even hear it. I answered.

"Oh, Alice," said Mrs. Sheavers from next door. "I just wondered what was going on at the Melody Inn tonight. I saw your father go out, and he was all dressed up."

I knew that Dad wouldn't want me to tell Mrs. Sheavers that he was going out with a woman named Elaine, but it wouldn't hurt for her to know that he had a date. Mrs. Sheavers would like to go out with Dad herself, because she and Mr. Sheavers are divorced too.

"He wasn't going to work," I said. "He's taking a woman to the symphony."

"Oh, well!" said Mrs. Sheavers. "That woman he works with? Janice somebody?"

"No. Someone else," I said. And then I added, "He has lots of girlfriends," which wasn't entirely true, but then, how would I know? He does know a lot of customers, and he would say that they are friends, and some of them are women, so it wasn't a lie, was it?

"I just wondered if something special was going on at the Melody Inn that I might like to attend," said Mrs. Sheavers.

Sure you did, I thought.

* * *

When Dad came home, Lester and I were waiting for him in the living room. I was sitting in my beanbag chair. I don't know what we expected—that Dad would walk in with Elaine on his arm, maybe, and say, *Well, kids, this is going to be your new mother,* just like Sara's dad may have said, *Let's move.*

Dad came in alone. He closed the door behind him and locked it. When he turned around, there we were, looking at him.

"Hellooooo!" said Dad. "You were expecting Santa Claus, maybe?"

"Just wanted to be sure you got home safe and sound," said Lester. "Have a good time?"

"As a matter of fact, I did," said Dad. And as he passed under the light in the hallway, I saw lipstick on the side of his face. Well, *somebody* was having a good year, I thought, even though it wasn't me.

4

The Party

Jody gave a sleepover Halloween party at her house. She invited three girls—Dawn, Megan, and me. She didn't invite Rosalind. We were supposed to come in costume, go out trick-or-treating together, and then come back for hamburgers and to stay all night.

Two of us would get to sleep in the bunk beds in Jody's room, and the other two would sleep on an inflatable mattress on the floor. Megan and I got the mattress, but that was okay.

Some of the girls, Jody and Dawn in particular, have been sort of mean to Rosalind this year, just like they were to Sara back in third grade. They talk about clothes and earrings a lot. They try to look like the girls in magazines.

Rosalind and I—and sometimes Megan—like to talk

about the same things Sara did. Elephants and bugs and volcanoes and ice-cream sundaes and ghosts and almost anything except clothes and earrings. And I don't look much like the girls in magazines, so I'm not sure how I got invited to Jody's party.

I never think about costumes either, until the last minute, and then I never know what to wear. The last couple of Halloweens I've just put on an old tuxedo jacket of Dad's and pretended I was anyone he said I was—a composer, a conductor, whatever.

This year when he got out the jacket again, he said I could be Mozart if I just wore a powdered wig, the way the men did back then. So we got a woman's gray wig at the dollar store and tied it in back with a black ribbon, and presto! I was Mozart.

Except that none of the other girls could figure out who I was, and they all tried to guess.

"Little Red Riding Hood's grandmother," said Dawn.

"No," I said.

"The old woman who lived in a shoe," said Megan.

I shook my head.

"The old woman who swallowed a fly?" asked Jody.

"No. Mozart," I said, careful to pronounce it correctly: "*Mote*-zart," with a *t* sound.

"Who's that?" asked Dawn.

"A guy who wrote music a long time ago," I said.

"Why would you want to be him?" Jody asked.

"It was Dad's idea," I said. I decided right there I would choose my own costumes from then on. That's what I got for being lazy.

We had a good time trick-or-treating, though. Almost everyone seemed to be giving out candy bars—the good kind—not those little boxes of raisins or those teeny packets of candy corn or gum balls. It was a cold clear night too, and we went four blocks up and down one street, then four blocks up and down another before we headed back.

We passed Donald Sheavers in a Batman costume, and then, under a streetlight, we saw Rosalind, walking all by herself.

"Hey. There's Rosalind!" I said to Dawn.

"Quick. Over here," Jody whispered, grabbing my arm and yanking us behind some bushes till Rosalind had gone by.

Somehow I'd thought that maybe Jody would call to her to come and join the party. Then I realized that Rosalind must have known there was a party and that I had been invited, because she hadn't said anything to me at school about trick-or-treating together.

When Rosalind was gone, we came out, and Jody said, "Boy, if Rosalind eats all her candy, she'll *really* be fat! You can already see her you-know-whats under her T-shirt."

"Breasts," I said. I hate it when people call parts of their bodies "you-know-what."

The other girls giggled.

When we got back to Jody's house, her mother had hamburgers waiting for us. We dumped our four sacks of candy in one big heap in the middle of the kitchen table, and then—one at a time—we took turns choosing something from the pile until the only things left were peppermints and pennies and toothbrushes from a dentist.

Afterward we watched a spooky movie on the TV in Jody's room, but it got too scary and we turned it off. I wondered what Rosalind was doing right then.

Last year Megan had a sleepover birthday party, and Rosalind had been invited that time. I thought she had been okay. If anyone was awful at that party, it was Megan's little sister, Marlene. She was bossing everyone around, telling them what to do and where to put the presents, and spying on us down in their family room.

"I wish you'd invited Rosalind," I said.

"She's too fat," said Jody.

"But she's funny and she's nice," I said.

Jody puffed out her cheeks and rolled her eyes, and Dawn laughed.

"When she gets to junior high school, she'll be sorry she ate so much," Jody went on. "In junior high you really have to look nice. Even your legs."

"Your legs?" I said.

"You have to start shaving," said Jody.

"*Shaving?*" I said. "Women *shave*? What's to shave?" This is what happens when you're the only girl in the family. When you don't have a mother, you don't know about important things like places where women have to shave.

"Haven't you noticed? There's hair on your legs, and it will get thick and dark as you get older," Jody told me.

After we'd put on our pajamas, we looked at our legs. Jody's hair was the darkest, so we could see fine dark fuzz on her legs. Mine was blond, and Megan's and Dawn's was sort of in-between. But none of it looked like hair to me. It looked like peach fuzz.

"So?" said Jody. "Do you want to practice shaving?"

"Uh . . . I don't know," I said.

Now Jody was really smiling. "I'll show you how," she said. She went across the hall to the bathroom and came back with four pink plastic razors and a can of shaving cream.

We all rolled our pajama legs up to the knees. Two of us sat on the bottom bunk with our legs propped up beside us, and the other two girls sat on the rug. "Okay, first you spray shaving cream all over your legs like this," Jody said. She was holding the can the wrong way and got shaving cream on Megan's hand.

"Oops!" said Jody. She tried again. This time she

sprayed the cream up one leg and down the other. She handed the can to Dawn, who did the same. Then she handed the can to me.

I held it just like Jody had done and sprayed a line of shaving cream from my ankle to my knee. Then I sprayed the other leg. It looked like a row of whipped cream on both halves of a banana split. All I needed was a cherry on top.

I handed the can to Megan, and all she got was a hiss of air. We had to scoop a little cream off our legs and give it to her.

"Now," said Jody, holding up one of the razors and taking off the safety clip, "you hold it like this, and then you run it along your leg."

We watched in fascination as the razor cleared a path through the shaving cream like a lawn mower cutting through tall grass.

"Feel," said Jody after she cut another path next to that.

We ran our hands over the path. Her leg felt very smooth.

"Now feel the other leg," said Jody.

We felt. It was fuzzy.

Jody continued to shave while we watched. I picked up one of the other razors, took off the safety clip, and tried to hold it like Jody was. I started at the ankle and made a long scrape up my leg. It hurt! Then I saw that

I had made a thin red line where the blade had cut me.

"Ouch!" I said, drawing back.

"You must have been pressing too hard or holding the razor wrong," said Jody. "You're supposed to do it gently."

"I didn't know that!" I said as blood trickled down my leg and onto the bedspread.

"I think you're supposed to wipe the shaving cream off first so you can see what you're doing," said Dawn.

Jody got some Band-Aids, and we stuck them in a row over the scrape. "I don't think I'll shave anymore," I said.

"Oh, you have to!" Jody said. "Once you start shaving, you have to shave for the rest of your life."

"*What?*" I cried.

"Once you shave, the hair grows back in real dark and coarse. That's the thing about shaving," Jody said.

"You didn't tell me that!" I gulped.

Jody shrugged and shaved her other leg. "Well, I'm telling you now," she said.

I stared down at my bandaged leg and felt like crying. Great. I would have one normal leg and one with a line of thick dark hair right down the front. I would be "Alice the Ape Girl" in high school. I would be "The Ape Lady" when I got to college.

Dawn and Megan didn't even try to shave. I was angry at Jody, but it was her house so I couldn't really say anything. We ate some more of our candy and brushed our teeth, and then Jody's dad came upstairs and blew up the inflatable mattress. Her mother gave us some sheets and blankets and pillows.

When the lights were out, we tried to see if we could name all the kids in our fifth-grade class, first and last names both. We got all the girls' names right, but we couldn't remember all the boys.

Then Jody started dividing the girls into two groups: the "Okay" girls and the "Huh-uhs." She'd name a girl, and then the other girls were supposed to say "Okay" or "Huh-uh." But when we got to Rosalind, I was the only one who said, "Okay."

Jody and Dawn looked at me sort of pitifully.

"You'd better not hang around with girls like Rosalind when you get to junior high, Alice," Jody said, "or you'll get stuck with her. Nobody else will want you around."

"*Why?*" I asked.

"You'll get a reputation. *Look* at her! Do you want to look fat like that?"

"But I'm not! Anyone can see! I just like her! She makes me laugh."

They gave me the pitiful look again. Even Megan did.

"In junior high you have to be careful how you look and how you dress and who you hang around with, Alice. It's important," Jody said knowingly.

"But what if you don't *want* to dress like everybody else and do what everybody does?" I said. "That's like being in the army! That's like being in prison!"

Jody shrugged. "Well, if you want to go your whole life without the right friends, it's okay with me," she said.

I knew I was going to stay friends with Rosalind no matter what. I knew I was going to invite her over even if she weighed five hundred pounds. I wondered if Jody was right about junior high school, though. It scared me to think I had to be like everyone else.

"Bor-ing!" I said aloud, but Dawn was laughing about something else, and nobody heard. As the other girls drifted off to sleep, I heard a soft hiss of air. Around two o'clock in the morning I realized that the mattress was deflating, and by six, when I woke up again, it felt almost as flat as the party.

5

A Comma Without a Tail

I didn't want anyone to see the long scrape on my leg. But when I went home the next day, I was reading the comics with my feet propped up on our big coffee table, and Dad said, "What did you do to your leg?"

I looked down and saw that he could see partway up my pant leg. I quickly set my foot on the floor. "Just a scratch," I said.

"I thought I saw a couple of Band-Aids up there, Al. Let me see what you've done," Dad said.

I think he worries about me more than most dads. Since Mom died, he probably worries about losing Lester and me.

"It's *nothing*, Dad!" I said, but that only made him more determined. Lester lowered the sports page and watched while Dad tugged at my jeans to find first one, then two, then three . . . four . . . five Band-Aids marching in a column up my leg.

"What did you do? Try to climb over a barbed-wire fence or something?" Dad said. "I need to know, because this could get infected if you cut it on something dirty."

"It was clean," I said.

"What was it?"

I took a deep breath and held it. "A razor," I said at last.

"A razor?" yelled Lester. "It wasn't one of mine, was it?"

"No," I said. "Jody was showing us how to shave our legs at the party."

"Hoo boy!" breathed Lester.

Dad stared at me. "You're only ten years old, for Pete's sake! What'll it be next?"

"Her armpits?" said Lester.

"Al, don't try to grow up too fast," said Dad.

"Don't worry, I won't," I told him. I didn't tell him I was going to develop a hairy leg and he'd probably have to put me in a freak show. One *half* of a hairy leg.

It was Rosalind who was *really* curious about what I did at Jody's, though. She came over that afternoon— Sunday—and we went to the playground to sit on the swings and talk, even though it was chilly out.

"How was the sleepover?" she asked. There was no

use pretending I didn't know what she was talking about. Rosalind knows everything.

"It was okay," I answered.

"Did you get a lot of candy trick-or-treating?" she said.

"Yeah. Did you?"

"Not too much. So what did you do at Jody's?" she asked.

"Ate hamburgers. Watched a movie," I told her. And then, because I knew she would find out somehow, I said, "Tried to shave our legs." I showed her where I'd cut myself.

"They think they're so grown up!" said Rosalind.

We were quiet for a minute, and I was afraid she'd ask why I'd gone to a party she wasn't invited to, so I said, "Want to come back to the house and I'll give you half my candy?"

"Okay," said Rosalind.

And then I was ashamed of myself. Rosalind needed friends, not candy. But I gave it to her anyway.

Mrs. Swick didn't look like she ever ate candy. She didn't look like she ate at all. When November came and she still hadn't laughed out loud once, Donald said he thought there was something wrong with her cheeks. Her lips. But I thought she looked sad. I walked by two teachers in the hall who were talking about her once, and I heard one of them say, ". . . such a shame."

When everyone went out for recess one day, I stayed behind and asked if she knew what had happened to a girl who should have been in our class this year, a girl named Sara.

"No, I don't," she said. She was sitting with her chin in her hand, staring out the window.

I waited. "I think they had to leave their house because they couldn't pay their rent," I said.

She turned and looked at me then. "That's really too bad," she said. "Was she a good friend of yours?"

"Yes. I thought we'd go all the way through school together."

Mrs. Swick gave me a little smile. "We don't always get what we want in this life, do we, Alice?"

"No," I said. "We don't."

Out on the playground I saw Mr. Dooley, our fourth-grade teacher, so I asked him about Sara. "Do you know what happened to her?" I said. "She was supposed to be in our class again this year, but she's not."

"I heard that her family went to live with a relative in North Carolina. Sara's grandmother, I believe," Mr. Dooley said.

"Then she's *not* living in a tent! She's *not* living in a car!" I said happily as he stared. "*Thank* you, Mr. Dooley!"

I went spinning around and around and went to find Rosalind. Then I spun her around too. "Sara's at her grandmother's," I said, and we both danced right there on the sidewalk.

That afternoon in class something strange happened. During math Mrs. Swick was calling on different students to go up front and put a problem on the board. Ollie Harris, a freckled guy, went up and so did a girl with glasses. But when Mrs. Swick called on Rosalind next, Rosalind just sat there with a strange look on her face.

"Rosalind?" Mrs. Swick said again. "Would you please go to the board and work out problem three?"

Rosalind just looked at her. Then she shook her head, got up, tied her sweater around her waist, and left the room.

We all stared. Rosalind had never done anything like that before. We looked at Mrs. Swick.

"Rosalind?" the teacher called. She got up and followed Rosalind out into the hall. From where I sat, I could see her talking to Rosalind. Mrs. Swick came back inside, but Rosalind didn't.

"Alice," Mrs. Swick said, "will you put problem three on the board and explain it for us?"

I was so worried about Rosalind, though, that I copied it wrong and had to do it over.

We finished math, but it wasn't until we'd opened our history books that Rosalind came back. I kept trying to get her attention, but she wouldn't even look at me. After a while Mrs. Swick called on Rosalind to read the next page, and after that, I guess, most of the kids forgot that she'd ever left the room.

When we traded spelling papers later, though, I asked, "What happened to you?"

"Tell you later," she said.

After the bell rang, when we were putting on our jackets, I asked her again. "Why did you leave the room?"

And she whispered back, "Got my period and I leaked."

"What?" I said.

Rosalind gave me a funny look, took down her lunch box from the shelf, and left the building.

I walked home with Donald Sheavers. Sometimes I do and sometimes I don't. Last year I wanted him to play a romantic scene from a Tarzan movie with me, but every time he tried to kiss me, I got the giggles. Finally he got tired of trying and went home. Now, when he wants to embarrass me, he thumps his chest and gives a Tarzan yell. If he starts doing that, I won't walk with him at all. If he acts halfway normal, I will.

"Sara's not living in a tent or a car," I told him. "She's staying at her grandmother's."

"She could be living in a tent or a car at her grandmother's," said Donald.

You never win with Donald Sheavers.

Lester was there when I got home. He had books piled all over the coffee table and was studying for a test. Oatmeal was at the other end of the couch sleeping.

It's Oatmeal who's growing up too fast. Growing old too fast, anyway. She's only two and a half years old, and all she wants to do is sleep. As I stroked her on the head and behind her ears, I wondered who I could ask about periods.

"Could I have Lisa's phone number?" I asked Lester.

"No," he said.

"Could I have Mickey's, then? I need to ask her something."

"What do you want to ask?"

I didn't think Lester could help me much. "Do you remember a long time ago when I asked you what a period was?"

"Yeah? What'd I say?"

"A comma without a tail."

"That's a fact," he said.

"Is there any other kind?"

"Ask Dad," said Lester.

I forgot about it until we were in the middle of dinner that night. "Dad," I asked, "what's a period?"

"Are we talking punctuation here?" said Dad.

"No. Rosalind said she got her period."

Dad glanced over at me. "Already? You do know about menstruation, don't you, Al?"

"Is that what Kotex is all about?" I asked.

"Yes. When girls get to be a certain age, they release a little blood a few days each month."

Release? Dad sounds so formal sometimes. I'd heard of releasing a prisoner or a herd of horses . . .

"You mean . . . like releasing floodgates or something?" I asked.

"Yeah, Al. When a girl gets her period, it's like the destruction of the Boulder Dam," said Lester.

"Les!" said Dad. "It's just a small amount of blood, Alice. Nothing to worry about."

"Then let's discuss another topic," said Lester.

But I wasn't through yet. "When will I get periods?" I asked.

"Maybe around twelve or thirteen," said Dad.

"Then why did Rosalind get hers?"

"Her body's maturing a little faster, that's all. Some girls may not begin till they're sixteen or older."

"Do boys get periods?" I asked.

"No."

"That's unfair!" I said.

"That's life," said Lester.

6

The Christmas Burglar

Every Christmas is the same since we moved to Maryland. Dad calls his father and brothers down in Tennessee to wish them Merry Christmas, or Uncle Howard and Uncle Harold call here.

Then we call Aunt Sally and Uncle Milt on Mom's side of the family, and we have to answer all Aunt Sally's questions, like are we eating right and is Lester running with the wrong crowd and am I having my teeth checked regularly and stuff. If Carol, their daughter, is around, we get to talk to her too, and that's the fun part. But mostly it's Aunt Sally who does the talking. She's Mom's older sister, and I know she promised she'd look after us when Mom died. Because we're in Maryland now, though, and she's in Illinois, that's sort of hard for her to do.

But this Christmas I was worried about my cat. Last year I could dangle a piece of ribbon in front of Oatmeal and she'd leap and twist around and bat at the ribbon, trying to catch it. Now she just looked at it. Sometimes she'd roll over on her back and swat at it with her paw, but she wouldn't jump.

"You're no fun anymore," I said, putting her in my lap and stroking her head. "What's wrong, Oatmeal?"

She settled down, but even her purr didn't seem as strong as it used to be. Sometimes when she followed me to the basement and then tried to go up again, she'd stop halfway on the stairs like she was out of breath. Now I tipped her head back and stared into her eyes. Green, like mine.

"Please don't die, Oatmeal," I whispered. "I couldn't stand it if I lost one more thing I love." She *won't* die, I told myself. And I didn't say a word about her to Dad or Lester.

We opened our gifts on Christmas morning in our robes and slippers. Every Christmas morning Dad makes pecan pancakes, and the rule is, we have to put something in our stomachs before we eat a lot of chocolate. But we can go the whole day in our pajamas if we want to, though we usually don't.

I gave Dad some new aftershave lotion so he would smell nice for Elaine, and I gave Lester some cologne from the dollar store so he could smell nice for Lisa.

Lester said thank you but did I mind if he returned it and got another kind, English Leather or something. I said it was okay with me if he'd rather smell like a horse.

Dad gave me a little pink radio and an overnight bag, and Lester gave me a denim pillow with ALICE embroidered on it in yellow yarn, with a yellow daisy for the dot over the i.

Then Dad made a roast, and when it was time for dinner, I mashed the potatoes and Lester made a salad. We'd bought a Mrs. Smith's coconut pie for dessert. We lit a candle for our table while we ate, and we played our favorite Christmas music, some we just heard a few nights earlier at the Messiah Sing-Along. Dad loves going to that every year, because he says Christmas is a time for music and caroling. I knew he wished I could carry a tune. Lester can carry a tune, but he didn't want to go caroling.

After dinner Dad went to see the woman named Elaine, and Lester went out too. He took Lisa Shane a present even though she doesn't celebrate Christmas. That left me alone on Christmas night, but I didn't care because I had a huge chocolate Santa all to myself, and I was enjoying every bite.

Dad said he'd be back by nine, and Lester said he'd be back by eleven. I was opening and closing the lid on a little basket of soaps that Aunt Sally had sent me when someone rang the doorbell.

I'm not supposed to open the door to anyone I don't know, and I'm especially not supposed to answer the door at night. If I turned on the porch light now, though, to see who it was and then didn't open the door, the person out there would know I was in here. So I just stayed where I was on the couch, sniffing each of the bars of soap, trying to figure what kind of flower each smelled like.

The doorbell stopped ringing at last, and someone began knocking instead. I didn't move a muscle. I didn't make a sound.

Finally the knocking stopped and I heard footsteps going away. I let out my breath and went back to smelling the soap again. I had just taken another bite of my chocolate Santa when I heard a noise at the back door. And then . . . *then* . . . I heard the back door open.

The door! I had taken out the garbage and the wrapping paper before dinner, but I'd forgotten to lock the back door again when I came in. The phone was in the hall. If I got up to call 911, the burglar in the kitchen would see me. Hadn't I heard that burglars go around on holidays looking for houses to rob while the families are out?

I heard slow footsteps coming across the kitchen floor. Maybe it wasn't a burglar. Maybe it was a murderer! The Christmas Night Murderer! I could just see tomorrow's headline: FIFTH-GRADE GIRL WITH MOUTH FULL OF CHOCOLATE FOUND FATALLY STABBED. I jumped up on my knees and had just swung one leg over the back of the sofa to hide when Donald Sheavers walked into the room.

I screamed anyway, just to let the fear out.

Donald jumped. "Jeez!" he said. "Calm down! Why didn't you answer the door?"

"Well, why are you creeping around at night?" I said, climbing off the sofa. "Where's your mother?"

"She sent me over with this," said Donald, holding out a German chocolate cake wrapped in cellophane. *To Ben from Harriett, with affection,* read the tag.

"Dad's not here," I said.

"Good," said Donald. "Want a slice?"

"What?" I said. "It's for *Dad!*"

"He's going to share it with you, isn't he?" said Donald.

"Sure, but . . ."

"So let's eat your piece now."

I noticed that Donald didn't say, *Why don't* you *eat* your *piece now.* But I got out a knife and two forks. I know I'm not supposed to have boys in the house when I'm alone, but I don't even consider Donald a boy. Donald is just . . . well, Donald.

"So what did you get for Christmas?" he asked me.

"A radio and a pillow and soap and stuff," I told him.

"Soap?" said Donald, scraping some frosting off his slice of cake and eating that first. "You stink or something?"

"You tell me!" I said.

Donald leaned over and sniffed at my neck at the same exact moment my dad came in.

"Donald!" he said.

Donald jerked to attention like a soldier.

"Al, what . . . ?"

"His mom sent over a cake, and I forgot to lock the back door, and he just walked in," I explained. "We're eating my share of it now."

Dad was still looking at Donald curiously.

"He was sniffing me to see if I needed any soap," I said. It gets very complicated sometimes, trying to explain Donald Sheavers.

Dad smiled then. He read the note. "Tell your mother thanks very much," he said to Donald. "I'll be saving some for Lester, too, because this is one of his favorites." And then he added, surveying Donald's plate, ". . . if there's any left."

After Donald went home, I figured I'd get a scolding about letting him come inside, but Dad just hung up his coat and sat down in his chair in the living room, staring at the Christmas tree lights. I went in and pulled my beanbag chair closer to him so that I was leaning against his legs and we could look at the tree together.

"Did Elaine like the present you gave her?" I asked. I didn't know what the present was, and I wasn't about to ask.

There was a long pause from Dad—so long that I didn't think he was going to answer. And then he said, "Well, she was gracious about it, anyway."

I sat straight up. "She didn't like it?"

"She has rather expensive tastes, I'm afraid. I think she was expecting something more."

"A diamond ring?"

He laughed. "No. I guess we're just from two different worlds, that's all."

"But . . . maybe . . . after you get to know each other better, she'll want to marry you anyway!" I said.

"It's a long road from friendship to marriage, sweetheart," Dad said. "Let's just say that Elaine and I wished each other Merry Christmas and Happy New Year, and let it go at that."

7

Running Away

One morning at school Rosalind opened the top of her desk to take out her geography book, and there, lying right on top of her things for all the class to see, was a sanitary pad with *Rosalind* written on it in red Magic Marker.

Rosalind dropped the lid of her desk so fast that it made a loud bang, and everybody jumped and looked around. I saw Jody and Dawn giggling together at the back of the room.

I had never seen Rosalind's face so red. We didn't know if any of the boys had seen the Kotex pad or not. Donald Sheavers did, I think. And if he saw, the other boys would soon know what was in Rosalind's desk.

"I just might run away," Rosalind told me at recess while the other girls were playing kickball with some of the boys to keep warm. All of them looked over at Rosalind from time to time and smirked.

I almost felt like running away with her. I never knew that fifth graders could be so cruel. Some of them were mean to me in third grade, and mean to Sara in third and fourth, but writing a name on a sanitary pad and leaving it in someone's desk was the worst thing yet.

"Where would you go?" I asked her.

"If I knew, I wouldn't tell you, because then they'd torture you until you told," she said.

"*Who* would?"

"The principal, maybe."

"Mr. Serio doesn't torture people!"

"The FBI, then."

"Rosalind, are you nuts?"

"Okay, but if I ever *do* disappear, I won't tell you where I am, but I'll be okay and will probably come back the next day. Only I won't tell anyone else that," Rosalind said.

I had two worries now: my cat and Rosalind. And I was keeping them both a secret.

Rosalind disappeared on Friday after school. It seemed like a normal day. Mrs. Swick never laughed, as usual, and I missed three problems in math, as usual, and Rosalind wanted to know if I had anything in my lunch we could trade, as usual. But about six that evening Rosalind's stepmother called our house and wanted to know if Rosalind was with me. She said that she had just come home from shopping and that Rosalind wasn't there.

My heart almost jumped out of my chest. Dad was holding the phone in his hand, waiting for me to answer.

"No," I said. "I don't know where she is."

Dad repeated what I said to Rosalind's mom.

"Did she say anything at all to you about where she might go after school? Mention any other playmate?" Dad asked me.

I shook my head.

"No," he said into the phone. Then, a few moments later, "Yes, please call us when she comes home. I understand how worried you must be, but—knowing these girls—I feel sure she'll turn up."

When he put down the phone, though, he said, "I shouldn't have said that. Knowing Rosalind, I'm not sure of anything."

I felt horrible knowing what I did about Rosalind's talk of running away.

Dad started making dinner. He opened a can of salmon and mixed it with an egg and cracker crumbs and celery, forming it into little cakes to fry on the stove. I sat on a kitchen stool, silently watching, the way I used to watch Mrs. Nolinstock cook our meals.

"It's pretty scary when you don't know where your kid is," Dad said.

He looked so worried that I heard myself saying, "She'll be okay."

He looked up. "How do you know that?"

I shifted uncomfortably on the stool. "I just think she will. Rosalind's pretty good at taking care of herself."

"After the trouble you two have been in, I don't believe that for one minute," Dad said, and turned the fire on under the skillet. "Her brothers are out looking for her right now."

I pressed my lips together hard so I wouldn't say anything more.

"Rosalind's mother is calling all her friends," Dad went on. "If nobody knows where she is, she's going to call the police."

"Will they call in the FBI?" I asked.

"Well, that depends. I wouldn't be surprised if they'd want to talk to you."

I swallowed. And finally I said, in a small voice, "Does the FBI ever torture people to make them talk?"

"What?" asked Dad just as Lester came in the door.

"What's this?" asked Lester.

"What on earth made you ask that?" Dad said to me.

"I just wondered if they'd torture me to make me say where Rosalind was even though I don't know."

"Of course not!" said Dad. "Even if you *did* know. *Do* you know?"

"No."

"Rosalind's missing?" asked Lester.

"Yes," Dad said, and told him about the phone call. They both looked at me hard. I could feel my cheeks turning pink and knew I was cooked.

"*O*-kay!" said Lester, putting down his books. He pulled out a kitchen chair, straddled it, and sat with his arms resting on the back. "Yes or no. Do you know where Rosalind is?"

"No," I said.

"Do any of your friends know?"

"No."

"Hmm," said Lester. Then I knew for *sure* I was cooked. "Did Rosalind tell you a secret?"

I didn't know how to answer. Running away was a secret. I couldn't lie.

"Yes," I said. Dad turned the fire off under the skillet and folded his arms across his chest. I felt like I had been arrested. Like I was being questioned by detectives. I felt as though they were going to make me sit up all night under a single lightbulb without food or water until I told them everything I knew about Rosalind.

"Alice," said Dad, "did Rosalind ever tell you she might run away?"

"Yes," I said, "but she said she'd be okay and that she'd probably come back the next day and that she wouldn't tell me where she was going so the FBI couldn't torture it out of me."

Dad tipped back his head and closed his eyes.

"For the love of Mike," said Lester.

Dad called Rosalind's mother and made me tell her everything I had told him and Lester.

"Why, Alice?" Rosalind's mother asked. "What was she so upset about?"

So then I had to tell her about how the girls tease Rosalind because they say she's fat and how they put a sanitary pad with her name on it in her desk.

"Thank you, Alice," said Rosalind's mother. "And thank you for being her friend."

It was a quiet supper. Dad and Lester didn't say too much, except that Lester said kids could be really cruel sometimes. I helped with the dishes, and Lester wanted to call Lisa, but Dad told him to stay off the phone in case someone needed to call us.

At a quarter of ten the phone rang. It was Rosalind's mother. She said that the custodian at the public library had found Rosalind hiding in one of the toilet stalls after the library closed and that the police were bringing her home.

I grabbed the phone away from Dad when he repeated that and begged, "Please don't punish her!"

And Rosalind's mother said, "I wouldn't dream of it. I think she's been through enough already."

I was glad that Rosalind had a nice stepmom. And I wondered if that would ever be me—with a stepmom who loved me that much, I mean.

8

Growing-up Stuff

No one at school found out that Rosalind had "run away." On Monday when they asked her where she'd been, because Rosalind's mother had called their mothers, she just said, "At the library." So everyone forgot, except Rosalind and me.

I asked Rosalind what happened after the police brought her home, and she said, "Nothing." So I didn't ask any more. But I noticed one change over the next week. There weren't any potato chips in Rosalind's lunch sack. There weren't any cheese crackers or candy bars, either.

There were pickles and peanut butter sandwiches and apples and pretzels and hard-boiled eggs. I wondered if it had anything to do with my telling Rosalind's mom that girls called Rosalind fat. I didn't talk to Rosalind about it, but I didn't trade any more food with her, either.

Around the first of February, Rosalind came to school with four invitations to a sleepover. She gave me mine first. "If the other girls ask if you're coming or not," she said, "say yes—that it's about secret grown-up stuff."

"Wow!" I said. "Okay."

The other girls seemed surprised to get an invitation. Jody looked as though she didn't know whether to keep it or throw it away. When we went out on the steps at recess and she asked if I was going, I said, "Sure! We're going to talk about secret grown-up stuff. *You* know!"

"Really?" said Jody. "Like getting your period?"

I nodded.

The thing about periods is that every girl who hasn't had one yet—all the rest of us—wants to hear about them. And because Rosalind was the first, we figured she could tell us everything we wanted to know. We knew that soon, in health class, we'd learn about stuff like this, but we wanted to know *now*. We wanted to learn it before anyone else did.

Because I said I was going, Jody said she'd go. And wherever Jody went, Dawn followed. Megan had to check with her mom first because she was in a piano recital and didn't know when it was. I called her that night to see if she was coming. Marlene, her bratty sister, answered.

"Is Megan there?" I asked.

"Who is this?" asked Marlene. Just like that.

"It's Alice, and I need to talk to Megan," I said.

"What about?" asked Marlene.

"It's none of your beeswax," I said.

"Then you can't talk to her."

If I had a little sister like Marlene, I'd want to throttle her. I don't suppose you can divorce a sister.

"If I have to come over there to talk to her, Marlene, there's going to be trouble," I said.

"Says who?" said Marlene.

Then I heard Megan calling, "Who's it for, Marlene?" There was a reply I couldn't understand and the sound of wrestling, and then Megan came on the line.

"Don't mind Marlene," she said.

"I just wanted to know if you were going to Rosalind's party," I said. "I hope so."

"Yes, I'm coming. Anything to get away from my sister!" Megan told me.

The girls were nice to Rosalind that week because they knew they'd be spending the night at her house. Rosalind didn't say a word about the Kotex pad someone had put in her desk. Maybe they thought she had forgotten, but who ever forgets something like that?

The more I thought about Rosalind's party, though, the more afraid I was that maybe she'd do something mean to the girls to get even. Or maybe her mother would scold them for the way they'd treated Rosalind.

But when we got to her house on Friday night, her mother was friendly and cheerful and had a huge bowl of popcorn waiting for us in Rosalind's room. We watched a video and painted our toenails raspberry red. Then we left our sleeping bags on the floor and crowded onto Rosalind's bed. Megan wanted to tell ghost stories, but Rosalind asked if we wanted to see a private book.

Private sounded more interesting than *ghost*, and we all said yes.

It was a thin booklet with a paper cover, and on the front it said: *A Girl Grows Up*.

It wasn't easy for the five of us to look at the book all at the same time, so Rosalind said, "You want to take turns? Each one of us can read a page aloud. This book is about *every*thing!"

Jody nodded eagerly, so Rosalind said, "I'll read the first page and you read the second." And she began: "'Congratulations! You and your body are about to change in new and wonderful ways. . . .'"

It didn't take long for us to realize that it was talking about menstrual periods. And since none of the rest of us had a book called *A Girl Grows Up,* we wanted to hear every word.

When it was Jody's turn to read, she put the book

flat on the bed so we could see the drawing that went with the page, showing what the inside of a girl looks like with all the parts included.

"It looks like a pear sliced open," said Megan, fascinated.

It pointed out things like ovaries and fallopian tubes, the uterus and bladder and vagina.

Jody read how the ovaries release an egg once a month, no bigger than a teeny-tiny dot.

"'The egg travels down one of the fallopian tubes to the uterus,'" Jody read. "'If there is sperm to fertilize it, the egg attaches itself to the inner lining of the uterus and will grow into a baby. If fertilization does not take place, the soft bloody lining of the uterus slides out the vagina once a month.'"

"What's the vagina?" asked Megan.

"The opening between your legs," said Rosalind.

"Oh." Megan looked confused. "I thought that's where you pee!" she said, then giggled and pulled the covers over her head. We all laughed and poked at her through the blanket.

"There are *two* places!" I said, because I knew that much. "One is the vagina and the other is where the pee comes out."

Now Rosalind poked *me*. "*Three* places! One where you poop," she said, and this time we all shrieked and stuck our heads under the blanket.

But it was Dawn's turn to read next. The booklet told how some girls use stick-on pads in their underpants to catch the blood, how some use tampons that you could insert into the vagina, and how these had little strings attached so you could pull them out when you needed to change them.

"Euuuw!" said Megan.

When we had finished reading the booklet, we passed it around again and again so every girl could see the drawings of what she looked like on the inside. It was awesome being in the same room with the one girl who had already started her periods.

"Does the blood come out all at once?" asked Dawn.

"No. It just sort of leaks out for three or four days," said Rosalind.

"How do you know when it's coming?" asked Jody. "What if you're walking to school when it happens?"

"You don't know exactly, but when it starts, it's just a little bit," Rosalind said.

"But what if you drip and you don't have a pad? What if you have blood in your pants by the time you get to school?" I asked.

"Then you go to the office or you tell the teacher, and she'll get a pad for you," said Rosalind importantly.

Dawn sat stiffly over by Megan. They all looked like soldiers going to war. "I'm going to put a pad in my backpack and have it ready at all times," she said.

"And an extra pair of underpants, too," said Megan.

The girls glanced over at Rosalind. I'll bet all of us were thinking that somebody might tease *us* the way they had teased Rosalind. That *we* might find a sanitary pad in our desks or someone might find one in her backpack. The classroom suddenly seemed like a dangerous place.

And then Megan asked the question that all of us were wondering about: "When there *is* sperm inside you to make a baby, how does it get in there?"

For a minute nobody said anything. We just looked embarrassed, because we had *some* idea of what happened between a man and a woman, but none of us knew exactly.

"I think the father squirts it up there," I said finally, which was about all I knew about sex.

"How?" asked Jody, joking. "With a spray bottle?" We all howled then, so hard that we rolled off the bed laughing.

When we climbed back on again, Rosalind said, "I think he puts it up there with his penis."

Megan clapped one hand over Rosalind's mouth as though she'd said a bad word, and then Dawn reached up and turned off the light. It was easier talking in the dark.

"He does *not!*" said Megan. "My folks would never do that."

"How, then?" I asked.

"The woman goes to the doctor, that's how," said Megan.

"The *doctor* puts his penis in her?" I asked.

"No!" Megan cried, and we all shrieked again.

"It's like Alice said," Rosalind explained. "The father puts his penis inside the mother. Dogs do it. Cats do it. Elephants do it."

"Well, *people* don't! It's gross!" said Megan.

We lay there in the dark thinking.

"Let's ask somebody," said Jody.

"Who's going to ask?" said Dawn.

"Alice," said Rosalind. "Alice will find out the answer and tell us Monday at recess."

"Why *me*?" I protested.

"Well, I already asked my mom for *A Girl Grows Up*, so it's somebody else's turn," said Rosalind.

"My mom doesn't even know about stuff like this," said Megan.

"Of course she does! She has children!" said Dawn. "I wouldn't ask my mom, though. I'd be too embarrassed."

"If I asked mine, she'd say, 'Why do you want to know?'" said Jody.

They all looked at me again. I swallowed. "Okay. Monday at recess," I said. That gave me exactly two days to find out.

Rosalind turned on the TV again, and we all pretended we were watching a video, but we weren't. I could see Rosalind looking at me on one side and Jody looking at me on the other, and this got us giggling again.

"I'll bet it's messy," said Jody.

"Maybe they do it in the bathtub," said Dawn. We giggled some more.

"Maybe they do it over the toilet," said Rosalind, and this time we laughed out loud.

Later, after the other girls had gone to sleep, I lay there thinking about sperms and eggs and Mr. Dooley's baby, back in fourth grade. If Rosalind was right, that meant that Mr. and Mrs. Dooley did it. That my own mother and father had done it. Doctors did it, and dentists and teachers and lawyers and even George Washington and Abraham Lincoln. Everybody who ever lived had got to this earth in the very same way.

It was sort of a miracle. I didn't think it was gross at all.

9

Love

By the time I got home Saturday from the sleepover, Dad had already left for work and Lester was getting on his bike to ride to his part-time job. It didn't seem like a good time to ask him about sperms and eggs, so I just said, "See ya," and he rode off down the driveway.

Oatmeal was waiting for me just inside the door. I think she misses me when I stay somewhere overnight, because she's been sleeping with me ever since she was a little kitten.

I went to the closet and got the belt off Dad's raincoat. I dragged it slowly across the floor. Oatmeal hunkered down the way she does when she's stalking something, and I was glad to see her looking more frisky. She crouched even lower to the floor, and the pupils of her eyes got larger and larger. She went skidding across the floor, chasing the belt.

I ran faster and faster—through the living room, the dining room, the kitchen, the hallway and back—and suddenly Oatmeal just stopped, her sides heaving. She sat there panting a moment, then walked over to the rug and lay down.

"Oh, Oatmeal. Don't grow old too soon!" I told her. She tipped back her head and let me stroke under her chin.

That night Lester browned the hamburger for chili, I cut up the green peppers and onions, and Dad made some corn bread. When we sat down to eat, I remembered what I was supposed to ask. But I didn't want Dad and Lester to think I didn't know *anything*.

"I know all about sex," I began. I saw Lester roll his eyes.

Dad looked up. "What?"

"I mean, you don't have to start at the beginning," I said. "You don't have to tell me everything."

"That's good," said Lester, "because I sort of wanted to talk about basketball."

I ignored him. "I know that it takes a man and a woman to make a baby, but I don't know exactly how the man gets his sperm inside the woman," I said.

"With a glue gun," said Lester, and took a bite of corn bread.

"Les!" said Dad. And then he cleared his throat.

I don't know why it is that I can't get a simple answer to a simple question instead of a lot of throat clearing and the whole history of the human race.

"When a man and woman want to start a family . . . ," Dad began.

"Please don't start with buying a house," I said.

"Yeah, Dad. Cut to the chase," said Lester.

So Dad speeded it up. "People who love each other want to get their bodies as close together as possible, and when that happens, the man puts his penis inside the woman's vagina."

"And out comes the sperm?" I asked.

"Something like that," said Dad.

"Like pee?" I asked.

"Not that much," said Dad.

"For crying out loud, I'm eating," Lester complained.

"Sounds messy to me," I said. I thought about it a minute. "Where do they do it? In the bathtub? Over the toilet?"

Lester bolted back in his chair. "I don't *believe* this!" he said. Then he hunched over his plate again. "They do it out in the backyard, Al, and hose themselves down afterward."

"Lester!" Dad said again. "She's asking some basic questions here. They do it in bed, Alice. People make love in bed."

"Oh," I said. "All over the sheets?"

"It's not as messy as you think," Dad said. "And what mess there is doesn't matter."

"Oh," I said again. I wondered if there was anything else the girls wanted me to ask. "How long does it take?" I asked.

"Just a few minutes or as long as a couple wants it to last," Dad said.

"Now, about those Boston Celtics . . . ," Lester began, and then he and Dad talked basketball.

As soon as the bell rang for recess on Monday, Jody and Dawn and Megan and Rosalind followed me around the school and back to the teachers' entrance, where we huddled together on the steps.

"Did you find out?" asked Jody.

I nodded and told them everything Dad had told me.

"I can't believe it!" said Megan, thinking, I guess, of her parents. "Then that's how they got my sister."

"And you," I said.

We sat in hushed silence.

"Let's don't tell anyone else," said Dawn. "Let's be the only girls in fifth grade who know."

"I just can't believe it!" Megan said again.

"It's how everybody gets born, Megan," I told her. "Mrs. Swick and Mr. Dooley, too. The principal! The president!"

"Moses, even!" said Jody.

"But not the pope," said Megan.

"Even the pope," I told her.

Dad told me later that sometimes when a woman has trouble getting pregnant, the doctor takes eggs from her and sperm from her husband and puts them together in a laboratory. And *then*, after an egg is fertilized, he puts it back in the woman and it grows just like any other baby. But I wouldn't tell Megan that because she'd say she was *sure* that's how she got born. Her sister, too.

Two days before Valentine's Day, Donald Sheavers asked if I was going to give him a present.

"What for?" I said.

"Valentine's Day. Because you're my girlfriend."

I had forgotten that I was supposed to be his girlfriend. Just because you're somebody's girlfriend one year, do you have to go on being it forever until you get a divorce or something?

"Oh," I said.

I went inside my house and sat down in my beanbag chair to think. I didn't want to be his girlfriend anymore, but it would seem rude to just tell him that. If I could find someone else to be his girlfriend, maybe it wouldn't be so bad. Now, who should it be?

Rosalind needed a friend, maybe. I called her up and

asked if she wanted to be Donald Sheavers's girlfriend.

"Sure," she said. "About as much as I'd like to break a toe."

I figured there was no point in asking the other girls about Donald. And I didn't really need to. All I needed was for Donald to believe that somebody else liked him, and then he wouldn't care if I was his girlfriend or not.

There was a pack of valentines beside my chair, ready to give out to the other girls in our class. I hadn't planned to give any to boys. I looked through the bunch. There were all kinds of valentines, from silly to mushy. I found a big red heart with lace around the edge. On the inside it said, *Crazy for You.*

I decided that instead of writing a girl's name underneath, I would put the first initial of three girls' names, and then Donald would never know for sure who had given it to him. So I took a pen and wrote *J* for Jody, *D* for Dawn, and *M* for Megan. I found an envelope for the big red heart, put the valentine inside, and wrote Donald's name on the front. At school, just before the party, I slipped it in Donald's box.

But I hadn't counted on Donald acting stupid. I hadn't counted on Donald being Donald. Instead of blushing a little and glancing around the room when he opened the envelope, Donald waved the valentine in the air and yelled, "Hey, who's JDM?"

All the kids turned around. I was sure glad I hadn't written any girl's name on that card. But Jody put down her cup of punch and said, "That's me!"

I stared.

"Jody Dianne Merwin," she said. "Why?"

Dianne? Her middle name was *Dianne*? I couldn't believe it. Meanwhile Donald was smirking. "I didn't know you were crazy for me," he said.

Jody snatched the card out of his hand. "I didn't write that!" she said.

I sank down lower in my seat until I almost disappeared.

"Who wrote my initials on this card?" Jody demanded, glaring around the room.

Saved by Mrs. Swick. "Let's don't make a fuss over this, Jody," she said, taking the card and giving it back to Donald. "If you didn't sign that card, that's all we need to know. Now, who would like more cookies and punch?"

I hung around after school because I didn't want to walk home with anybody. I didn't want to show my face in the classroom again until everyone had forgotten the valentine party. Jody would be furious if she knew I had given Donald that card. I asked Mrs. Swick if I could help clean up the room.

"Why, thank you, Alice," she said. "I'd appreciate that. Could you take a damp paper towel and wipe off the desks? Some of them are a little sticky."

I wished I could do one nice thing on Valentine's Day. I wished I could go home and say that I had made Mrs. Swick laugh. So while we were working, I told her all about Oatmeal and the way she would crouch down and tremble when she was about to pounce on something. I told her how my cat used to jump high in the air when I dangled a string. Mrs. Swick smiled, but she didn't laugh.

When I went outside, though, Donald was still there, reading all his valentines on the steps. He got up and gave me a little bag of valentine candy, the kind that has words stamped on the hearts—HI, BABE and HOT STUFF and I DIG YOU.

I had to tell him: "I don't have anything for you, Donald," I said. "I don't think I'm your girlfriend anymore. Sorry."

He took the candy back and broke open a corner of the packet. He popped a piece in his mouth. "How come?" he asked.

"Because we're not in love or anything," I said. "I'd just rather be friends."

"Okay," said Donald, and he ate the rest of the candy.

Lester still had the same girlfriend, though. Last year at this time he got in a lot of trouble because he stayed out later than he was supposed to on Valentine's Day. And I got in trouble because I turned off the alarm clock that Dad sets outside his room on the nights that Lester is out. It's set for the time Lester's supposed to be home. If he's not home in time to turn it off, it wakes Dad up and then there's trouble.

When Lester came home from school, I said, "I'm not going to turn off the alarm clock for you tonight, Lester."

"So who asked you to?" he said. "Lisa and I celebrated early. I'm not going over there tonight."

"Did you give her a present?" I asked.

"Naturally."

"Did you *kiss* her?"

"Knock it off, Al."

I climbed up on a stool in the kitchen and watched while Lester made himself a sandwich. "I'm not Donald Sheavers's girlfriend anymore," I said, "so I didn't give him anything." And then I asked, "Do you think Dad will ever get married again?"

"Hope so," said Lester.

"Because I don't think he's going to marry Elaine. I asked him this morning if he was taking her out tonight, and he said no."

"Well, some things take time," said Lester.

"If I knew what kind of a wife he was looking for, maybe I could find someone for him," I said.

"You can't do that, Al. It doesn't work that way," Lester told me.

I thought about that for a minute. "What was Mom like? *She* must have been the kind of woman he was looking for."

"She was funny. Natural. She didn't dress up a lot. She liked music, same as Dad. She used to sing a lot, too."

"She looks beautiful in her pictures," I said.

"She was nice-looking. Pretty, maybe, but not beautiful."

"Well, if I ever *do* find a woman like that, I can at least tell Dad about her, can't I?"

"The surest way to ruin a romance is to set two people up," said Lester. "People like to find each other on their own. They don't want other people to do it for them."

I decided right then that if I ever met a woman I thought Dad might like to marry, I would secretly arrange for them to meet, and I'd never, ever, let them know I'd planned it. I *especially* wouldn't tell Lester.

The phone rang, and I thought for sure Lester would pick it up, but he said, "Go answer, will you? And if it's Mickey, tell her I'm not here."

"I'm not going to lie, Lester," I said.

He grabbed up his sandwich and went down the hall to the bathroom. "Okay, then. If it's Mickey, tell her I'm indisposed," he said. He went inside and shut the door.

I picked up the phone. It was Mickey. "Is Les there?" she asked.

"He's indisposed," I told her.

"Meaning . . . ?" said Mickey.

I wasn't exactly sure what it meant either. "He's in the bathroom," I said.

"Oh. I'll wait," she said.

Now what was I supposed to do? "It might be a long time," I said.

"He's taking a shower?"

Showers only lasted so long, I thought, and she was willing to wait. She'd *never* hang up.

"I think he's on the toilet," I said. "He may be there a long time."

Mickey giggled. She always giggles when she finds out personal things about Lester. "Is he sick, or is it something he ate?" she asked.

Now I'd really done it. If I said he was sick, she'd ask him if he was better. "No, it just takes Lester a really long time," I said.

"Well, when he comes out, *if* he comes out, tell him his devoted valentine is sending hot burning wishes his way."

No wonder Lester doesn't like Mickey, I thought. After I hung up, Lester came out of the bathroom.

"Mickey said that when you come out, *if* you come out, I should tell you that . . ." And then I wasn't sure.

". . . that your burning hot valentine sends devoted wishes your way . . . or something."

Lester rolled his eyes. "How'd you get her to hang up? That's usually a twenty-minute job."

"I said you take a really long time."

"You said I was in the shower?"

"I said you were on the toilet."

"Al!" he bellowed, grabbing up a newspaper and charging at me. He chased me down the hall to the bathroom, and I ducked in and locked the door. Then I stayed for a very long time.

10

Big Mistake

The first day of March, I fell on the playground. The day was warm, and we'd all taken off our jackets and coats and left them in a heap on the concrete steps.

Donald Sheavers and the other boys were teasing the girls. They named each girl and said what boy she was in love with, and Donald said that once I asked him to come over and kiss me, which was a big fat lie. Sort of. I had asked him to come over and play a scene from Tarzan, which had a kiss in it. But we never actually did.

And then Ollie said he wanted to play Tarzan with me, and I jumped up and started to run across the playground, and then Rosalind was running with me, and then there was a whole pack of boys chasing us, all thumping their chests and making Tarzan yells.

I hated Donald Sheavers just then for telling them about that. I hated that I was running and that Ollie Harris and Cory Schwartz and all the other boys were chasing us. I hated that it looked like we *wanted* to be chased and kissed. Lester told me once that when a boy tries to kiss me, I should just turn around and chase *him* and that would scare him to death. But when it's a whole bunch of boys, *then* what do you do?

This was third-grade stuff! I shouldn't have run at all. When Ollie said he wanted to play Tarzan with me, I should have just given him a look and said, *Yeah, right!* But it was too late now. The only thing left to do was duck in the teachers' entrance and escape, but then I realized I had run right by it.

I skidded around to go back, but one foot went out from under me on the gravel and I fell right there in the parking lot, sliding along on my right arm.

Everyone stopped running then, including the tribe of girls who were running after the pack of boys who were running after Rosalind and me. There was a big raw place on my right arm.

"Oh!" Rosalind said when she saw it.

"Euuuw!" cried Megan and Dawn, and the next thing I knew all my solemn-faced girlfriends were ushering me through the forbidden teachers' entrance, and the boys hung back, looking sheepish.

Down the hall we went to the office, girls hanging on

to me on both sides. They turned me over to the school secretary, each one giving her account of how the boys had chased me and I fell. Then they went out, looking back at me sorrowfully, and I was alone with Miss Otis.

We don't have a nurse at our school. If one of us has a temperature, Miss Otis calls our parents. If it's an emergency, of course, she'd dial 911. But if it's only a bump or a scrape or a cut or a bruise, Miss Otis takes care of it herself.

"Wow!" she said when she looked at my arm. "Now that looks nasty, doesn't it?" She guided me into the little room just off the office. It has a sink in one corner, a cot, a blanket, a basin, and a chair. She led me over to the sink.

"Now, this is going to hurt a little, Alice," she told me, "but we've got to get the dirt out. I'll be as gentle as I can." Her brown eyes searched my own, and her brown shoulder-length hair brushed against my cheek. She had almond-shaped eyes and skin that always looked tanned, even in winter. She was new to our school this year, and all the boys called her sexy.

I gritted my teeth and tried not to look as she washed my arm with soap and water, but she made me laugh a little the way she kept saying "Ouch" for me. Her fingers were long and slender, and her nails had rose-colored polish on them.

When the wound was all cleaned out, she examined my arm again. "It's really not a deep scrape, but sometimes these shallow cuts and scrapes bleed like crazy," she said.

She had me sit down on a chair next to the cot while she put some ointment on the wound. After that it didn't hurt as much. It was when she was wrapping a bandage loosely around my arm that I thought what a kind and beautiful stepmother she would make.

I watched her as she taped the bandage. She didn't look anything like the pictures of my mom. Mother's skin was freckled, and her hair was strawberry blond, like mine. Miss Otis reminded me more of a green olive than a strawberry, but my dad likes olives, too. I decided right then that I was somehow going to arrange for Dad and Miss Otis to meet each other.

At lunch all the girls wanted to sit next to me, and they cast angry glances at the boys' table. But while I was eating my cheese and cucumber sandwich, I was thinking of all the reasons Dad could come here to school and meet Miss Otis. Back-to-school night had already come and gone, and unless I got into real trouble, Dad wouldn't be called to the office. Even if he was, it would be to talk with Mr. Serio, our principal, not Miss Otis.

The only thing I could think of was my arm. I might never be sick again the rest of the year. This might be my only chance. So that afternoon, around two'clock, I went up to Mrs. Swick and told her I didn't feel so good.

"Really?" she said. "Is it your arm?"

I nodded. "I think maybe it's infected," I said.

She put her hand on my forehead. "Are you sure this doesn't have something to do with math?" she asked. She had just told us to do all the problems on page forty-seven.

"No, it really hurts," I said. "Maybe I'm going to throw up."

"Then if you're feeling that sick, you'd better go back to Miss Otis," she said. "Dawn, would you please walk her to the office?" Teachers always do that when you're sick—ask another student to walk with you to make sure you don't faint on the way or something.

Dawn put her arm around my waist, and I moaned a few times as we went down the hall. She gave me a pitying look and left me just inside the door.

"Now what?" Miss Otis said when she'd finished talking with someone on the phone.

"I don't feel so good," I said. "I think maybe you ought to call my dad to come and get me."

"Are you feeling warm or what?" Miss Otis asked.

"Sort of like I might throw up," I told her.

When Miss Otis took me in the sick room this time, she sat me on the cot and placed the basin on the floor between my feet. I wondered how many other kids had thrown up in this very basin and imagined pink and green and brown stuff splattering all over their shoes and socks.

"Did you just now start feeling this way?" she asked.

"No, it was right after I hurt my arm. I think it's infected," I said.

She looked at my arm again. "Oh, I don't think so."

I remembered how Dad acted when he saw that scrape on my leg after I'd tried to shave it. "You'd better call him," I said. "He told me he needs to know when I get hurt."

She studied me seriously for a minute or two. "Did you hurt your head when you fell, Alice?"

"I'm . . . not sure," I said.

"Okay. Is your father at home or at work?" she asked.

"Work. He's the manager of the Melody Inn Music Store," I said. "He knows everything there is about music."

"Hmm," she said. But finally she went back to her desk and looked up my folder. Then she called the Melody Inn.

I couldn't hear what she was saying because some kids came in the office just then and they were arguing about something and Mr. Serio was scolding them. Finally, though, Miss Otis hung up and came back in the sick room.

"Alice, your dad says he can't get away just now because he has to fill in for a violin instructor, but he's going to call the high school and have your brother come by to pick you up."

"No!" I said. This was working out all wrong.

"High school lets out in twenty minutes, Alice. He'll be here soon. I think you can hold out until then," she said.

I lay down and closed my eyes and tried not to think of throwing up for real. For the next half hour I listened to people coming in and out of the office, the phone ringing, teachers talking, and—at last—Lester's voice. I couldn't make out what he was saying, but he seemed to be taking his time getting in here.

Finally he followed Miss Otis through the doorway and looked down at me.

"Hey, meatball," he said. "How you doin'?" He reached for my arm and looked it over. "I don't see any red streaks. No gangrene."

I didn't answer.

"Well, I've got my bike outside. Think you can hold on long enough for me to get you home?"

Wordlessly, I got up from the cot. Miss Otis had sent someone for my jacket, and Lester helped me put it on.

"Thanks," he said to Miss Otis. And then he added, with a twinkle in his eye, "And any time *you* want a ride on my bike, just give me a call."

She laughed. "I'm afraid my boyfriend would have something to say about that."

She had a *boyfriend*?

"Darn!" said Lester, smiling at her again. And then, turning to me, he led me outside and over to his bike.

"Hop on," he said, holding the bike steady while I climbed up on the bar and grabbed hold of the handle-bars. Then, swinging one leg over the seat, Lester got on, and a minute later we were careening out the school driveway, past the crossing guards, who didn't even try to stop us.

"Man!" said Lester. "That Otis babe is *hot*!"

"Oh, shut up, Lester!" I said. "Just shut up."

11

A Very Dark Day

By the time April rolled around I decided that fifth grade was just a joke. One of my best friends had moved away, there was an ugly scrape on my arm, I was going to grow up with a hairy leg, and Miss Otis already had a boyfriend. If I ever got a stepmom, it would probably be Mrs. Sheavers, and the only thing worse than waking up each morning to find her making pancakes would be to find Donald sitting at our table eating them.

Lester's life was going okay, though. He had already applied to Montgomery College for the fall semester, Dad was going to buy him a used car as a graduation present, and the senior prom was coming up in May. He had been saving his money and was making plans for where he and Lisa would go after the prom.

It takes a lot of money to go to a prom, and Dad wasn't very sympathetic, I could tell.

"In my day," he said one evening at dinner, "we bought the tickets, the corsage, borrowed our dad's car, and took our dates to the Chicken Basket first for dinner. Nobody rented a tux, nobody rode in a limo. . . . It's ridiculous, Lester."

"So tell that to Lisa!" Les said. "What do you want me to do on prom night? Take her to McDonald's?"

"I already told you that you could use my car. A limo will put you back . . . what? A couple hundred?"

"We're going in with two other couples on the limo, and Lisa's paying for the photographs," Lester said.

"Well, in my day—"

"This isn't *your* day!" Lester said impatiently. "When you were dating, did you always do whatever *your* dad had done when he was in high school? I don't think so! Times change, Dad."

Dad chewed silently for a minute or two. Finally he said, "You're right. But when I think of all the things the money could buy . . ."

"Let me have this one night without having to think of all the things the money could buy," Lester said.

"Fair enough. But I want to know your complete plans for the evening, Les. I'd like to be able to go to sleep that night without worrying."

"That's why we're renting a limo, Dad, so you

won't have to worry about our driving," Lester said.

Dad wasn't the only one who was worried about Lester and prom night, though, and it wasn't just about his driving. On Sunday, when Dad and Lester went out to look at used cars, Aunt Sally called from Chicago.

"Alice, sweetheart, how *are* you?" she asked.

"Okay. Dad's fine and so is Lester," I said, knowing that's what she'd be asking next. "They're out looking at used cars. It's going to be Dad's graduation present to him."

"Oh, my! He's growing up, isn't he?" said Aunt Sally.

"We're all growing up," I told her.

Aunt Sally always saves her most important question till last. When she was quiet a moment, I knew she was worried about something.

"I suppose Lester's going to the senior prom?" she said.

"Yes. He's taking a girl named Lisa, and they're going to rent a limo," I said.

"Oh, gracious!" Aunt Sally said. "Has he talked to your dad about it?"

"About the limo?"

"About *everything*."

"You mean, about sperms and eggs?" I said.

"Oh, my goodness, Alice, you're only in fifth grade!" she said, flustered. "Well, I was calling because there was this article in our paper about high school proms and about the things that go on, even in limousines!" she said. "I just thought your dad should know."

I was curious. "Like what?"

"Well, some limousines, Alice, have Jacuzzis in them."

"Jacuzzis? You mean, hot tubs?" I said.

"Would you believe it?"

"You mean, people take a bath on the way to the prom?" I tried to imagine it.

"Well, I don't know about a bath, Alice, but you can hardly get in a Jacuzzi with your clothes on, so that can only mean one thing."

"That they're taking off their clothes in the limo," I said.

"And you're not too young to be told that once you take off your clothes, anything can happen."

"I know," I said importantly. "Like fertilizing an egg."

Her words ran right over mine, she was so breathless. "So tell your father that I called and that he should make sure Lester doesn't rent a limo with a Jacuzzi in it."

"I'll tell him," I said.

As it happened, Dad and Lester didn't find any car they liked enough to buy, so Dad dropped Lester off here at home and then went back to the Melody Inn to do some paperwork.

Lester came in and got a Pepsi from the fridge.

"No luck?" I said.

"We were just doing some pricing, seeing what's out there," Lester said.

"Just don't buy a car with a Jacuzzi in it," I said, grinning.

"Huh?"

"Aunt Sally called, and she's worried you're going to rent a limo with a Jacuzzi."

"Is she nuts?" said Lester.

"She's worried you'll take off your clothes."

Lester laughed. "As a matter of fact, we are. We're renting a pool at a Holiday Inn after the prom, and about thirty of us are going to have a swim party when the prom's over."

"Just make sure there's no fertilizing going on," I told him.

On Monday, I was walking home from school beside Donald Sheavers, and he said that Killer, his dog, was blind now. The dog's real name is Muffin, but they keep a water dish on their back porch with the name "Killer" on it so if a burglar comes by, he'll think there's a vicious dog inside.

"How does he find his way around?" I asked.

"With his nose," said Donald.

"How old is he?"

"Twelve," said Donald. "That's old for a dog."

"What if he loses his sense of smell? Then what happens?"

"I guess we'd have to carry him around wherever he wants to go," said Donald.

I went on up the walk to our house, and Donald went next door to his. I took the key from around my neck and opened the door. Then, dropping my book bag on the couch, I went out to the kitchen for a snack.

Oatmeal was lying in her favorite spot of sunshine, and I stepped over her to get a vanilla pudding from the fridge. Oatmeal likes it when I choose vanilla because I let her lick out the container when I'm through.

I got a spoon and pulled the tab off the top of the pudding. Usually this makes her sit up and walk over. But Oatmeal didn't move. I looked down at her, lying there in the sunlight. She didn't seem to be breathing. Her sides didn't rise and fall.

"Oatmeal?" I said, dropping the spoon and crouching down on the floor beside her. Her mouth was half open. So were her eyes. The pupils were glassy.

I couldn't breathe for a moment myself. I put my hand on her body. It was stiff. I screamed. I stumbled out on the porch and just stood there, screaming.

The screen door banged next door.

"What's wrong?" asked Donald.

"Oatmeal!" I cried. I just kept screaming it. "Oatmeal!"

Donald ran over, but I could hardly see him through the tears. It wasn't fair! Donald had a dog. Muffin was so old, he couldn't see and it was probably time for him to die, but Oatmeal was still a young cat!

And suddenly I started beating against Donald Sheavers' chest with both fists.

"It isn't fair!" I wept. "It's just not fair!"

12

Hating the World

I didn't know if I was more sad or angry. Mrs. Sheavers had heard me screaming and came hurrying over, but I rushed back inside and locked the door and wouldn't let her in. When Lester came home, I was still in a rumpled heap in a corner of the couch—Oatmeal's corner. I cried until the arm of the sofa was wet and stained.

Mrs. Sheavers had stopped him outside and told him about Oatmeal. When Lester came in, he just sat at the other end of the sofa and watched me cry. I only quit because I was too tired to cry anymore. He reached out and lightly touched my ankle, but I jerked my foot away.

"Sometimes," Lester said, "life really stinks."

"It's not fair!" I yelled again, as though it were all his

fault. "Muffin should have died instead! Even Donald's had a longer life than Oatmeal did!" I paused a second, realizing what I'd said. "Why do bad things happen to *our* family? Why do they have to happen to *me*?"

"I don't think there *is* a why, Al. Sometimes they just do." He was quiet a moment, and then he said, "I know how you feel, though. I felt the same way when Tippy died."

I remembered Lester's dog then. The way he ran across the street once to greet Lester and got run over. I was real small then, but I still remember how they rolled Tippy's body up in a rug and put him in the trunk of our car.

"I'm angry at God too!" I went on. "If He can't even keep a little kitten alive, what good is He?"

"Yeah, I felt that way too."

"He couldn't keep Mom alive, He couldn't help Sara's family pay the rent, He—"

We heard Dad drive up just then, and I knew immediately that Mrs. Sheavers had probably called him at work and told him what happened.

"Honey, I'm so sorry about Oatmeal," Dad said when he came in, and that started the tears all over again.

Lester went down in the basement to look for a box to bury her in, and Dad took his place on the couch. I crawled down to Dad's end and curled up against him.

"It's my fault," I wept.

"Now, why do you say that?"

"Because I knew something was wrong with her. She wasn't as frisky as she used to be and . . . and sometimes when she was r-running, she'd just stop and pant," I said. "But I didn't tell anyone. I was afraid of what it might mean."

"I think we all knew that she was slowing down, Al. You remember when we took her to the vet for the first time? And he said she was fine except for a heart murmur? He told us that a lot of kittens outgrow that, but some of them don't. It was just something she was born with, and we'd have to wait and see."

I sort of remembered and sort of didn't. I remembered the way Oatmeal kept pouncing at the vet's fingers there on the examining table while he was talking. And I think I remember Dad asking me if I wanted to take her back and trade her for another kitten in the litter, but of course I didn't. This was the one Dad had picked out for me, and that made her special.

"Well," Dad said, "Oatmeal just turned out to be one of those kittens who didn't outgrow it. And her heart condition got worse. There was nothing we could have done, but think of the happy life we gave her while she was alive."

That didn't help. "Why does everything in this family die?" I wept angrily. "First Mom and then Tippy and then Uncle Charlie and now Oatmeal?" Who would be next? I wondered. "I'm mad at God," I said again.

"I know."

"He could do *anything* if He wanted! How much work would it take to heal a little kitten's heart?"

Dad patted my shoulder. "Maybe that's not His job."

"Well, if He can't give us what we want, what's He there for?" I said.

"Maybe to help us get through the times we *don't* get what we want."

I didn't want to hear it.

"It's not what happens to us, Al, that's nearly as important as what we do about it," said Dad.

"What am *I* supposed to do about it?" I said angrily. "*I* can't bring back Oatmeal!"

"No, but you can let something like this make you angry at the world or you can let it make you a better person somehow."

I didn't want to hear that, either. All I wanted was my cat back. All I wanted was to hold her and hug her and feel her scratchy tongue on my hand.

"It's probably too early to talk about this, but we can get another kitten," said Dad.

"No!" I said, sitting straight up. "I don't want another cat. I don't want anything else I love to be taken away." Lester, I remember, had said the same thing after Tippy died.

"All right," said Dad. "But it's okay if you change your mind later."

"I *won't!*" I said. "Don't bring me another kitten, Dad. Promise me you won't do that."

"All right," he said.

Lester came back upstairs with the box that his running shoes had come in. I crumpled up old newspaper and put it in the bottom of the box to make it soft. Then we put Oatmeal's little blanket on top. Dad picked up Oatmeal's body and placed her gently on the blanket. Crying, I put her favorite toy between her paws.

"O-Oatmeal," I sobbed, and stroked her head one last time. But I couldn't really see through my tears.

Lester put the lid on the box and taped it shut. Then Dad got his shovel, and we went out on the back step.

"Where do you think we should bury her?" he asked me. "Next month that azalea bush by the fence will be in bloom. Do you want to bury her under that?"

I nodded.

"Do you want to ask any of your friends to come over?"

I shook my head.

I held the box while Lester cleaned some of the weeds away from under the azalea bush, and then Dad thrust his shovel in the ground and began to dig. I heard a screen door slam and turned around to see

Donald and his mother standing out on their steps, watching.

"Tell them to go back inside," I muttered.

"Now, Al, there's no reason to be unkind," Dad said.

"Well, life isn't being kind to *me*!" I shot back. I glared at Donald and his mother, and after a while they went inside.

Dad dug down about two feet, and when the hole was wide enough, I knelt down and placed the box at the bottom.

"Maybe we'd each like to say something special about Oatmeal," said Dad.

"I . . . I *loved* her!" I said. "When I picked her up the first time, she was the softest thing in the world."

"I liked the way she jumped up and crawled into my lap when I read the newspaper," said Dad.

"I liked the way she'd eat my creamed spinach," said Lester. I knew he was trying to make me smile, but nothing could make me smile.

"Well . . . ," Dad said finally, and lifted the shovel again.

"Wait!" I said. There were some wild violets growing here and there in our yard, and I picked a handful of the best and sprinkled them over the box. Then another handful. And then I went inside while Dad filled the hole.

I was looking for some kind of marker I could put on

Oatmeal's grave. Her toys were scattered around the house, and I chose a little gray rubber mouse that looked so lifelike, you'd think it was real. I stuck it on the end of a shish kebab stick from the kitchen drawer and took it outside. Then I stuck it in the dirt above the grave.

But there were reminders of Oatmeal everywhere. Her food dish, her water dish, all the other toys. There was even her hair on the end of the couch where she liked to sleep and hair on the blanket on my bed.

"How do you ever get over losing something or somebody?" I asked my dad that night.

"You don't, Alice. You go on remembering them forever until they just become a part of you. And finally you discover that the good memories are the ones that stay with you, and you can let the sad parts go."

In bed that night, my first night without my cat since third grade, I tried to remember only the good things about her and not the ways I had noticed she was slowing down. But I wished I had been with her that afternoon. I wished I had been sitting on the floor in her patch of sunlight, stroking her head. I couldn't stand the thought that she died alone.

I was angry at myself for not being there. I was angry at Donald because he came over. I was angry at his mom for watching, at Muffin for being alive, at Sara for not telling me that her family was leaving. . . .

I guess I was mad at anyone who had a pet, anyone who had a mother, anyone who had a best friend. I was afraid that *I* might turn into a Mrs. Swick someday for real—the girl who never laughed.

❀ ❀ 13 ❀ ❀

Real Trouble

I didn't want to go to school the next day, but Dad wouldn't let me stay home. I wouldn't walk with Donald, though. I waited till he'd gone, and then I set out, my eyes straight ahead. I didn't even go over to where Rosalind and the other girls were talking by the swings.

When the bell rang and I went inside, Rosalind and the others caught up with me. "What's wrong with *you*?" she asked.

"Oatmeal died," I told her.

"Oh no!" said Rosalind. "What happened?"

"It was her heart. She had a defect."

"Why didn't you have it fixed?" asked Rosalind.

People say the stupidest things sometimes. How was *that* supposed to make me feel?

"Because we *couldn't*, Rosalind! Not everything can be fixed, okay?" I shot back.

The girls put on their sad faces, but I saw them glance at each other before I turned away. When I scraped my arm, I wanted them around to comfort me; now I didn't.

At lunchtime, though, the girls tried to be extra nice.

"Sometimes," Megan said, "a whole lot of bad things happen at once to somebody. My uncle was in a car accident, and the next week Aunt Sharon had an operation and almost died. And then their garage caught on fire."

"My mom knows a woman who had four children, and three of them died when they were babies," said Jody.

"Maybe God was sending a message," said Dawn, and stuck her straw down inside her chocolate milk carton. We all looked at Dawn.

"What kind of a message?" I asked.

"Like the plagues in the Bible," said Dawn.

"You mean the woman who lost three children is being punished?" asked Rosalind.

Dawn shrugged. "I don't know. Maybe." She sucked hard on her straw.

Rosalind looked at Dawn, then at me, and back at Dawn again. "Do you think *Alice* is being punished?"

"I don't *know*!" Dawn said uneasily. "I just remember

what we learned in Sunday school about God sending the plagues."

"You know what *I* think?" I said, a little too loud. "I don't think God is fair, that's what! And I don't know if He's so great if He can't even keep a little kitten alive."

All the girls gasped, even Rosalind.

"Oh, Alice, you'll go to hell!" said Megan.

"So what?" I snapped.

They gasped again.

Miss Burstin, our third-grade teacher, was on lunchroom duty. She'd heard Megan say "hell" and moved closer to our table.

The girls finished eating, took their trash over to the garbage cans, then went on outside. I took a long time eating my bag of pretzels because I didn't care if I had any playground time or not. I didn't feel like playing.

When I went outdoors finally, the girls had cornered Dawn over by the fence.

"That was a stupid thing to say," Rosalind was telling her.

"You shouldn't have said that to someone who just lost a pet," said Jody, and that really surprised me.

They turned and looked at me as I walked up. "Well," I said, "someday maybe *her* cat will die, and then she'll know how it feels."

"Yeah!" said Rosalind.

Dawn started to cry. I just turned and walked away, and the other girls went with me.

Every morning I got up and saw Oatmeal's hair on my blanket. I felt angry. Angry and sad.

I gathered up all of Oatmeal's toys, put them in a plastic bag, then took Dad's shovel and dug another hole in our yard. I put the toys in there and covered them up so I never had to see them again.

To make matters worse, I was having a hard time with math. I hated story problems. They never sounded like real problems to me.

Farmer Brown has two acres of lima beans. He has five men to pick them. If each man does an equal amount of work, how many square feet of lima beans will he have to pick?

"This is stupid!" I yelled. "I'm not a farmer! I don't have any lima beans! I don't even like lima beans. Why do I have to do stupid problems like this one?"

I was trying to do my homework at the kitchen table, and Dad was washing pans in the sink.

"Okay, let's pretend that it's another problem, Al," he said. "Let's say that your rich aunt left you two pounds of pearls. You are feeling generous and want to share them equally among you and your three best friends. How would you go about doing that?"

"I don't have a rich aunt," I grumbled.

"So? Answer my question."

I thought about it. "I'd have to figure out how many ounces each girl would get," I said.

"And how would you do that?"

"Know how many ounces are in a pound."

"And . . . ?"

"Well, if there are sixteen ounces in a pound and I multiply by two, I'd know how many ounces there were altogether. Then I'd divide that number by four girls."

"Right. So how do you find out how many square feet of land each bean picker would have to work?"

"I'd have to know how many square feet are in an acre," I said grudgingly.

"Okay. See? If you think of the same kind of problem in simpler terms, sometimes that will show you how to do it."

I finally finished the story problems and thought I was all done with homework. Then I realized I had a paper to correct.

Check the spelling, Mrs. Swick had written beside a word in my paper about our community. I had written *resterant.* It looked okay to me.

"How do you spell 'restaurant'?" I asked Dad.

"Look it up," he said.

I trudged into the living room and took our dictionary off the shelf. I looked under the *r*'s. There was no *resterant*. I tried *restorant*. That wasn't there either. I tried *resterint*. But that wasn't listed.

I dropped the dictionary on the floor and gave it a kick. "How are you supposed to look a word up in the dictionary if you can't spell it?" I bellowed. "School is stupid! Teachers are stupid!"

Dad came to the kitchen doorway. "Al, pick up that dictionary and put it back on the shelf," he said.

I reached down, picked it up, then shoved it back on the shelf so hard that all the other books fell over and two dropped off the end.

"Cut it out!" Dad said. "You're making the whole family miserable."

"Good!" I said. I picked up the two books and put them back on the shelf. Then I went down the hall to my room and slammed the door. Hard.

When I got enough money, I decided, I was going to get a T-shirt that read, DON'T MESS WITH ME on the front. I would wear it all the rest of fifth grade. When it got dirty, I'd wash it and dry it overnight and put it on again the next morning.

I didn't smile all the way to school the next morning. I glared at the crossing guard. I barked at a little kindergarten kid who stopped just inside the door to tie his shoe and almost made me fall over him. And when I went home that afternoon, Mrs. Sheavers was taking some bags of groceries out of her car and a bag ripped open. Cans of tomato sauce and some onions fell to the sidewalk.

I didn't offer to help. I didn't even say hello. I just went on in the house.

Sometimes I hate the way I'm acting, but I just can't seem to stop. If I was walking down the street and met a girl like me, I'd tell her to go jump in the lake and take her frown with her. It just seemed as though everyone else in the world was happy but me. Everybody else had something nice to think about, and all I could think about was Oatmeal.

I'd only been inside for five minutes when the phone rang. It was Dad.

"Al, I just wanted you to know we're at Holy Cross Hospital. Lester broke his leg riding his bike home from school this afternoon, and he's on his way over to X-ray. I don't know when we'll be home," he said.

✿ ✿ 14 ✿ ✿

A Great Idea

I walked over to my beanbag chair and sank down. It made a loud *squish* when I landed, like all the air going out of my lungs at the same time. If I'd had a blanket, I probably would have sucked my thumb.

My brother had broken his leg. The brother who was supposed to go to the prom. The brother who had been working part-time at a miniature golf place to earn enough money to take his girlfriend in a limousine.

Maybe he'd ruined his bike, too, and maybe his condition was worse than they thought. Maybe he'd broken more bones than they suspected. What if he'd banged his head and had amnesia and wouldn't recognize Dad and me?

I couldn't sit still, so I got up and walked back and

forth between the kitchen sink and the front door, worrying about Lester. I decided the best thing I could do for Dad and Lester was to have dinner ready when they got home. I looked in the cupboard and found a can of macaroni and meatballs and a tin of sardines. I looked in the refrigerator and found some cheese and lettuce. I looked in the freezer and saw some ice cream.

Rosalind called and asked if I got the fourth problem on page sixty-two, and I told her that the fourth problem on page sixty-two was the last thing on my mind right now and that I didn't care if Farmer Brown sold his lima beans or not.

"That's not the one," said Rosalind.

"I don't care. There's a family emergency going on right now, and I'm too busy to talk," I said.

I set the table. I opened the macaroni and meatballs and put them in a microwave dish. I set the sardines on a saucer and got down some crackers for the cheese. Then I cut the lettuce into small pieces for salad and put a little dish for ice cream at each plate.

Dad and Lester didn't get home until seven. As soon as I heard the car drive up, I ran out on the steps.

Dad got out and went around to Lester's side. He opened the rear door and took out a pair of crutches. Then he opened Lester's door and helped him stand up. Slowly, Lester hobbled round the car, his lips tight and his face tired.

I held the door open for them. Lester didn't seem to know how to use crutches yet, and they swung wildly to the sides as he came up the steps. They clunked against the railing when he reached the top, Dad right behind him in case he fell.

I didn't know what to say to someone who had just broken his leg, so I said, "How's your leg?"

"Just wonderful, Al. Never better," Lester growled.

"It turned out it's his ankle, Al," said Dad.

"Oh," I said. "Then it's not so bad, is it?" And when Lester gave me a look, I said, "I've got your macaroni and meatballs ready."

"Huh?" said Lester, and hopped up the last step.

"I guess it's a good thing you don't have amnesia," I told him.

"Al . . . ," said Dad, so I shut up.

Lester managed to make it to a chair in the kitchen before he dropped his crutches on the floor with a loud bang. I saw the corners of his mouth turn down, the closest I had ever come to seeing Lester cry since he got to be a teenager.

"I'm really sorry about your ankle," I told him.

"There goes the prom," Lester said bitterly. "This just ruins everything!"

Nobody said much at the table. I guess there wasn't much to say about the food anyway. Each of us got a big spoonful of macaroni and a meatball and a half, four sardines, and some lettuce and cheese and crackers.

"This is all?" asked Dad, looking around.

"There's ice cream in the freezer," I said hopefully.

"This stinks," said Lester. "This ankle stinks. Life stinks."

"Yes," said Dad. "Sometimes it does. But it could have been so much worse, Lester."

What happened, I found out, was that Lester's bike skidded going around a corner, and when he fell over, his foot was still clipped into his pedal. All Dad could think about was what might have happened if Lester had fallen over in front of a car.

He said that until Lester could get up and down stairs without crutches, he could sleep in Dad's bed and Dad would sleep in the basement.

"How am I going to do that?" Lester said. "All my clothes are in the basement. All my stuff! My books and CDs and—"

"I'll be your fetcher, Les," I said brightly. "Just tell me what you want, and I'll go get it for you."

"That's nice of you, Alice," said Dad.

But I saw tears in Lester's eyes no matter how hard he tried to hide them. "All I wanted was to take Lisa to the prom, and now I'm going to have to tell her it's all off," he said, and turned his face away.

I spent the evening getting things for Lester. I went

up and down the basement stairs so much that my legs ached. When I finally fell into bed that night, I discovered that when I was doing something for Lester, I wasn't so sad about Oatmeal. I didn't forget her; I could never forget her. I just didn't think about her all the time when I was worrying about someone else.

I didn't like the person I had been the last few days, I decided. I wanted to be the girl who had stuck up for Rosalind when the other kids were mean to her, the girl who had wanted to help Sara, the girl who had tried to make Mrs. Swick laugh, and the girl who was kind to Lester. I didn't know that other girl who wanted to be mean to the whole world, and yet I knew she was part of me too.

The next day at recess I was sitting on the steps with Megan and Jody and Dawn and Rosalind. Dawn and Jody were looking through a teen magazine, trying to find a new way to fix Jody's hair, which hung down over her eyes like a sheepdog's. I'm not too interested in hair. Lester says he's seen me try only two ways to fix mine: combed and uncombed.

They knew I didn't want to talk about hair, not after my brother had broken his ankle. Megan thought we all ought to take some Magic Markers and draw flowers and happy faces on his cast, but somehow I didn't think that would cheer him up.

I was sitting next to Dawn, hugging my knees and feeling sad, when suddenly I yelled, "Stop!" and grabbed hold of the magazine.

The girls stared at me and then at the open page. There were pictures of unusual prom outfits for guys and girls. There were dresses and tuxedos that looked like they were made of animal skins. Clothes that had been put together with duct tape. Tuxedos with fur collars to wear in cold climates and dresses to wear when it was hot. And right there at the bottom of the page was a picture of a girl in a bikini top and a teeny-tiny skirt and a guy in a tuxedo top and satin shorts. *Cool fashions for a hot climate!* it said beneath the picture.

Yes! I thought. Lester could still go to the prom with his ankle in a cast if he could just slip on a pair of red nylon shorts over his cast. I told the girls about my idea, and Dawn said I could take the magazine home and show it to Lester.

Lester hadn't gone to school that day because the pain medicine had made him oversleep, and Dad said he could take one day off to rest up. I was afraid maybe he had already called Lisa and told her he couldn't take her to the prom.

"Wait!" I yelled as I burst through the door.

Lester had been asleep on the sofa and almost fell off. "What the heck?" he yelled.

"I've got an idea! A really great idea!" I said. "You can go to the prom after all."

"You're crazy," said Lester. "I couldn't even get into a tux."

"But you could get into a pair of shorts," I said. "Look!"

I opened the magazine to the pictures of crazy prom costumes. I pointed to the photo of the guy in a white tuxedo jacket. He was wearing a fancy white shirt with ruffles down the front and a red bow tie. There was a carnation in his lapel. And he was wearing red satin boxer shorts.

The boy in the picture was a real hunk. He was handsome as anything. He had big muscles in his legs. Lester looked at the photo a long time.

"Even if I could manage that getup, I couldn't dance," he said. And then he added, "Of course, nobody really goes to dance in the first place, I guess."

"Yeah!" I said. "I'll bet kids just go to show off and see what everyone else is wearing!"

The phone rang and I ran over to get it. I brought it back to Lester because the calls are almost always for him. There was a girl's voice at the other end, and it wasn't Mickey's.

I went out in the kitchen and made myself a graham-cracker sandwich with a hot marshmallow in the middle. I made one for Lester too.

When I took it out to him, he smiled at me. It was the first time he'd smiled since he broke his ankle. "Hey, Al," he said. "You're all right."

"Thanks," I said. "So are you going to the prom after all?"

"I'm gonna try," he told me.

15

One Dead Beetle

The doctor said that Lester would need to use crutches for a few weeks but that he could probably put his weight on the cast by the night of the prom.

"If you wear red satin shorts, Lester, I could draw red hearts all over your cast," I offered.

"No, thanks," said Lester.

"I could go along and bring you stuff all evening," I said. "Punch and cookies and things."

"No, thanks," said Lester.

"I could ride along in the limo with you and make sure you don't take off your clothes and get in a Jacuzzi," I said, grinning.

"Uh . . . no, thanks," Lester said again. "Don't press your luck."

Lester was feeling better and so was I. My eleventh

birthday was coming up on May 14, and because Lester was sick last year on my birthday, Dad promised me a party for this one. I was afraid that maybe because Lester broke his ankle, I couldn't have a party this year, either. That maybe he'd go on getting sick and breaking a bone every year around my birthday so I could never have a proper celebration again. But Lester said no, that as long as my friends didn't kick his leg or jump on his cast, a party would be fine.

"What kind of a party do you want?" asked Dad.

"My whole fifth grade?" I said.

Dad gave me a look. "How about the same kids you invited to your birthday last year," he suggested.

That was okay. I got out my silver sparkle markers and some index cards and made invitations for Rosalind, Megan, Jody, Dawn, Ollie, Donald, and Cory Schwartz—all the people I knew best. But there was one person left, and that was Sara. I guess there is always a hole—an empty place in your life—where a friend has been.

We held my party on a Sunday so that Dad wouldn't have to take time off work to be here. He said he would be in charge of the refreshments if Lester would be in charge of the games. And because I'd helped Lester find a way to go to the prom, Lester said he would be master of ceremonies.

First, he said, everyone had to come in costume.

"Lester, this isn't Halloween!" I protested.

"Everyone has to come in a color," said Lester. "One color. They can choose any color they want, but everything they put on has to be the same color."

"Even their underpants?" I cried.

"Except their underpants. Tell your friends I won't be checking underpants."

"So then what happens?" I asked.

"The person who does it best gets a prize."

"What's the prize?"

"I haven't thought of it yet," said Lester.

At four o'clock on Sunday afternoon I was dressed in green, from my head to my toes. I had on a green T-shirt with dark green frogs all over it, green shorts, green socks, and old green sneakers. Lester was all in white: white T-shirt, shorts, one white sock, one white sneaker, and the white cast on his other leg. Dad was busy in the kitchen, so Lester said he didn't count.

Most of the kids came in just one color, except Megan, who didn't have any shoes that were pink. Jody won the prize—a bag of M&M's—because she'd chosen blue and everything about her was blue, even the polish on her nails. Dad lined us up like paints in a paint box and took a picture.

"Okay, listen," said Lester. "Here's the deal. I'm going to send you on a scavenger hunt, and you've got to be back here in forty-five minutes."

"What's a scavenger hunt?" asked Ollie. "How do we know where to find it?"

We laughed.

"A scavenger hunt is where you look for stuff on a list," said Lester. "I'll give you the list. After forty-five minutes I'll go out on the steps and ring a cowbell. You can go one block in either direction, and you have to go in groups of two or three. Nobody goes off by himself. The group that comes back first with all the stuff on the list wins. But *everyone* has to come back when they hear the cowbell. You can knock on people's doors and tell them you're on a scavenger hunt, but you can't go inside. Got it?"

We quickly teamed up. Ollie and Donald and Cory went together; Rosalind and Megan chose me, so Dawn and Jody were a team. Lester gave each group a copy of the list and a paper bag.

"On your mark, get set, *go!*" said Lester.

The boys went up the street, Jody and Dawn went down, and Rosalind and Megan and I stood out on the sidewalk reading the list.

In honor of Alice's eleventh birthday, it said at the top of the page, *collect the following eleven objects:*

1.   *One dead beetle*
2.   *A peanut butter sandwich*
3.   *A dirty sock*

4. *A clean Band-Aid*
5. *An old toothbrush*
6. *A dill pickle*
7. *A baby's pacifier*
8. *A candy wrapper*
9. *Lip gloss*
10. *A black shoelace*
11. *Something gross*

We giggled and started off. Some of the things were easy to get, like the Band-Aid and the dill pickle. But other things—the lip gloss and pacifier—could be a problem.

The three of us went up to each house together.

"Excuse me," one of us would say when someone opened the door. "We're on a scavenger hunt. Would you happen to have a dirty sock?"

Everyone laughed when they read our list.

"I could give you one, but I'm afraid I might not get it back," one woman said.

And a man said, "I'd take the sock off my foot, but the smell would knock you out. What's next on your list?"

"A peanut butter sandwich?" asked Rosalind.

"No problem," the man said with a laugh. And we waited on his porch while he made one for us. Rosalind wanted to eat half, but I wouldn't let her.

At the next house we got a candy wrapper and a black shoelace, and we found a dead beetle beside the steps.

"Let's go to Donald Sheavers' house for the dirty sock," I said, and Mrs. Sheavers laughed when she opened the door and heard what we wanted.

It was one of Donald's, and it was dirty, all right. Smelly, too.

"Do you think this would do for something gross?" Megan asked as we went back down the sidewalk. But then we saw something even more gross. Somebody had stepped on a worm, and half of it was squished flat.

"You pick it up," said Megan.

"No. You," I told her.

Rosalind picked it up. The worm fell apart. The squished half fell back to the sidewalk, and the other half wiggled a little in Rosalind's hand.

"Euuuw!" Megan and I said together.

"Worms are like that," said Rosalind. "You could even cut one in two and it would turn into two worms."

I never know whether to believe Rosalind or not.

When Lester rang an old cowbell, we had found everything on the list except the lip gloss, the old toothbrush, and a baby's pacifier. No one else had found a pacifier either, but Ollie and Donald and Cory got the most.

What we all wanted to see, of course, was something gross. Jody and Dawn had found a dead mouse, but the boys got something even worse. A woman had been cleaning out her refrigerator and gave them a container she'd found far at the back. When Ollie took off the lid, we couldn't tell what it was, but it was covered with green mold and smelled like a dead animal.

"Euuuw!" we all said, and held our noses, and Donald and Ollie and Cory got the prize—little fold-up binoculars you could fit in a pocket.

Dad made a good dinner for us. We ate out in the backyard and had a hot-dog buffet. Dad had all kinds of stuff we could put on them: onions, pickles, relish, ketchup, cheese, and pineapple.

Then we had an ice-cream buffet, with chocolate sauce and chocolate chips, nuts, coconut, and M&M's to put on top. There was cake, of course. And beside the cake was an envelope addressed to me. It had *Happy Birthday* written across the envelope in green letters. It didn't look like Lester's writing, and it certainly wasn't Dad's.

"What's this?" I asked.

"I don't know," Dad said. "It came in the mail yesterday, so I saved it for the party."

Lester was cutting the cake, and Donald was begging for the piece with the most frosting. The girls were lined up waiting for theirs.

I sat down on one of the lawn chairs and opened the envelope. It was a homemade birthday card, with silly little people across the top, all gobbling up cake. I smiled because it was exactly what we were doing now. All the people on the card had big eyes and big ears. They looked almost like bugs. *Have a good birthday, Alice!* it said on the card. *If I were there, I'd give you a goldfish, because my grandmother has too many. So this will have to do. Sara.*

I looked in the envelope again. There were the remains of some Goldfish crackers, only they were mostly crumbs.

"It's from Sara!" I said happily, waving the card at Rosalind. Under her name there was an arrow pointing to the back of the card. I turned it over:

Dear Alice,

We are staying at my grandmother's until we see if my dad's job is going to work out in Texas. Then we'll probably go there. My grandmother's house isn't very big, but we like it anyway. She has two dogs and about a million fish. I hope you have a great birthday. If Rosalind is there, give her an elephant kiss for me and keep one for yourself.

Love,
Sara

P.S. To give an elephant kiss, blow water through your nose.

16

Thinking of Mom

I think that the card from Sara was about the best present of all.

Everyone brought me something, of course. Donald Sheavers gave me some of his comic books, Ollie gave me a jar of jelly beans, and Cory gave me a flashlight. From Megan and Jody and Dawn, I got a bead set, a headband, and a tiny purse, but Rosalind gave me a purple clay elephant. It was about three inches long, made in India, and had green and gold and pink spangles embedded in it.

"I bought it for you at the zoo," she said.

I told her I was supposed to give her an elephant kiss from Sara, but Donald was the only one who tried to do it. He tipped his head back and poured ginger ale in his nose, and then he tried to sneeze it out. All the girls jumped up and got away from him. Ollie and Cory just laughed. Boys can be so gross sometimes.

"Okay," Dad said, smiling and handing Donald a napkin. "Anybody want more cake?"

Donald did. So did Cory.

"I was born at four in the morning," said Dawn.

"I was born right at midnight," Jody told us. "The doctor said I could probably say I was born on either the day before or the day after."

"Mom says I came at six in the evening," said Ollie.

"When were you born, Alice?" Jody asked me. "Are you officially eleven years old yet?"

I didn't know what time I was born, and Dad had gone back in the house. Mom never told me, and now I didn't have a mother to ask.

"It was a great party, Alice," Dawn said when parents drove up later and kids started to leave.

"Yeah, we had a lot of fun," said Megan.

I helped Dad bring in all the stuff from the backyard— the blankets and paper cups and soda cans.

"What time was I born?" I asked him as we washed the bowls and spoons and forks.

"Quite late at night, as I remember," he said.

"Did I take a long time?"

"Nope. You were a pretty speedy baby. Lester took a lot longer, being the first."

"Were you with Mom when I came out?"

"Yes, I was right there. Could have caught you in my bare hands if I'd been quick enough, but the doctor was quicker. They wouldn't let me in the delivery room for Lester, and I wanted to make sure I was there for you," Dad said.

"What did I look like?"

"Well, to tell the truth, you looked like a piece of moldy cheese."

"Dad!"   ·

He laughed. "Till they cleaned you up, that is. Then we thought you were the most beautiful baby girl in the whole world."

"Was Mom happy that I was a girl?"

"I don't think I'd ever seen her more happy."

"I wish she were here," I said in a small voice. "I wish she could see me now."

"I wish it every day of my life," said Dad. "But especially on your birthday."

Lester was hobbling in from the other room singing "Happy Birthday." "Okay, Al, close your eyes!" he called out.

I did. "Don't put anything gross on me, Lester," I warned.

"Happy birth-day, dear Alice . . . ," he sang, coming closer. I felt something go around my shoulders. I felt something touch the top of my head. "Happy birthday to you!" he finished. "Okay. Open your eyes."

Lester was standing in front of me holding a hand mirror. I looked. I was wearing a gold crown made of cardboard and a cheap shiny gold cape.

"What *is* it?" I said, laughing.

"Queen for a day, of course! Except that you can keep them and wear them as much as you like."

I took off the crown and examined it. Lester had taped my name over some printing on the front. I peeked underneath and read MINIATURE GOLF QUEEN, TAKOMA PARK, MARYLAND.

"Les-ter!" I grinned. "I'll bet you got this stuff for free."

He ignored me. "And now, for your subjects . . . !" He took down a plastic fishbowl from the top of the refrigerator, in which he had arranged sand and seaweed or something. There, swimming around inside, were two of the tiniest fish I had ever seen. The larger one was fat and gray-green; the smaller one was every color of the rainbow. .

"They're so *tiny!*" I said. "What are they?"

"Guppies," Lester said. "The female—the larger one—gives birth to about fifty live guppies every month or so. Keep that up, and you'll have a vast kingdom in there."

I'll have to admit that Lester's present was original. I liked the thought of something reproducing in front of my very eyes, especially now that I knew how reproducing was done, though I'm not sure if it was quite the same way for guppies.

"Ah, yes. I believe I have a little present for you too," said Dad. He went back in his bedroom and returned with a small package. Dad doesn't pay too much attention to wrapping paper. He says it's all he can do to get it around the box in the first place. This time he had wrapped the present in Christmas paper, and there were rows of red and green snowmen running from left to right.

"Way to go, Dad!" said Lester.

I unwrapped and opened the box. Inside was another box, this one made of wood. The lid was decorated with carvings of parrots and a jungle motif around the edges. It must have taken a long time for a carver to make that box. Inside were two ten-dollar bills and a note that read, *Happy birthday, Alice. Love you. Dad.*

"Thank you," I said, taking out the money and examining the box some more. It didn't look new, and I figured there was a story behind it somewhere. "Was it Mom's?" I asked.

"Not quite. It was a present from her to me. I've been keeping my cuff links and tiepins in it. But I thought now that you're past your tenth birthday, you might like to have it. Because she chose it for me, you know that your mom picked this out herself. It must have been something that caught her eye, that made it special. And maybe you'd like to keep special things in it."

"Juicy love letters and stuff," said Lester, grinning.

"You're really giving it to me?" I asked Dad, surprised. Worried, maybe.

"She actually gave me two, Alice, and I'm keeping the smaller one. But I think she'd be very pleased to know I gave you this."

I wasn't sure what I would put inside it. Maybe I could choose some small thing from each year of my life.

"Thanks, Dad," I said, giving him a hug. "You too, Lester."

I liked going around all evening wearing my cape and crown. I sat on my bed later with the carved wooden box on my lap, tracing the parrots with my finger and thinking about the mother who had bought this special box, how her fingers must have traced the same deep-cut lines.

I needed something really special to put in the box, and I chose Sara's birthday card. It just fit. A special letter from a special friend inside a special box on my eleventh birthday.

17

News

"I have some rather important news," Dad said after dinner the following night.

Lester and I both looked up from our veal chops. When we have veal chops for dinner, you know that Dad did the cooking.

"You and Elaine are getting married after all?" I asked.

"No, Al. I'm not even seeing her anymore," said Dad.

"You're buying me a *new* car? A Mustang?" asked Lester.

"Sorry, no. I've been thinking for some time that we really should be buying a house, not renting. Rent is just money down the drain that we could be putting toward a purchase. So I've been doing some looking off and on, and recently, a two-story house came on the market that interested me. It's in Silver Spring, much closer to my work, and I liked it so much, I made an offer on it this morning."

"You did?" exclaimed Lester. That *was* news! Les and I looked at each other, not very sure of what this would mean.

"I have to leave all my friends?" Lester said next.

"Les, you'll have a car soon, and it's only about fifteen or twenty minutes from here."

Lester brightened.

"But *I* don't have a car," I said, not even sure if I was sad or excited.

"No, but we can still arrange for you to come back here for a day now and then. Maybe you could stay with the Sheaverses," said Dad.

"Not the Sheaverses!" I protested.

"Besides, you'll be making lots of new friends over there, because you'll be going to a different school if we get the house," Dad said.

I liked the idea of a bigger house, but I didn't like the thought of a new school. I liked the idea of new friends, but I didn't want to leave Rosalind. But when Dad said, "So . . . the real estate woman said she'd be at the house at seven tonight if you want to take a look at it," I was in the car in thirty seconds. Lester wasn't far behind.

It *was* exciting, and I decided to be The Girl Who Is Having a New Adventure. Something new was happening, and I was part of it. Maybe the house would be really nice. Maybe the new school would be great. I wouldn't have to walk to school with Donald Sheavers anymore.

"We still have a full basement in the new house," Dad told Les as we rode down Georgia Avenue, "so you can still have your drums down there."

"I've been thinking of selling my drums," Lester said.

"Really?" said Dad.

"Yeah, I think I'm more into guitar now."

I wondered if Lester was trying to get more money to spend on Lisa at the prom.

Dad went past the Melody Inn, turned at the corner, drove a few blocks, and turned again. The business section gave way to houses, and the shady trees made a roof over the streets. The houses were a little bigger than our house in Takoma Park. Some even had porches. I always wanted a porch.

The car slowed down, and Dad stopped in front of an ordinary-looking white house with a front porch and dark green shutters on the windows. There was a big tree in the front yard. I could see several more in back. It wasn't a beautiful house. It wasn't ugly. It was one of the smaller houses on the street, actually, but it looked like home.

The real estate woman was waiting for us and got out of her car when we pulled up. She was pretty and sort of young, and I saw Lester brush back his hair when he saw her.

"I'm still waiting for a call from the owners, Mr. McKinley," she said to Dad. "I phoned them your offer this morning."

Dad introduced us, and we followed her up the steps to the porch, a wide wooden porch with an old glider at one end. I tried to imagine how it would feel to live there. If these were *our* steps, *our* glider, *our* porch.

Inside, the living room was a lot bigger than the one we had now. The rooms were empty—the people had already moved out—and our voices had a hollow sound when we called to each other from room to room.

I raced upstairs because I wanted to see which room would be mine. I liked having an upstairs and a down-stairs.

"Which bedroom would be mine?" I yelled back at Dad.

"I'd like the large one at the rear, but you and Lester can duke it out for the other two," Dad said.

Lester wanted the bedroom with all the built-in bookshelves, and that was okay with me, because I liked the one with green and white wallpaper. Downstairs, the kitchen was big and old-fashioned. It had high cupboards that reached the ceiling, and everything was old—the stove, the sink, the refrigerator. But it looked out over a big backyard.

"I love it, Dad!" I said. "I really love it!"

"I guess it's okay," said Lester, coming up from the basement on his crutches. "Okay" is about the most excited he gets about anything. "Lots of room down there."

"Well, it's not ours yet," said Dad. "I don't want you to get your hopes up. I offered about the most we could afford. But if this doesn't work out, we'll get a house somewhere else."

I didn't want another house, I wanted this one. Maybe it was because it was the first house I'd looked at, but I wanted to eat in that kitchen, sleep in that bedroom, sit on that front porch.

When we got home, Dad said we should stay off the phone in case the real estate woman tried to call us. Lester sat on the couch, his physics book on his lap, his foot in its cast propped on the coffee table. I sat in my beanbag chair, trying to do my math problems. Dad was in his chair reading the newspaper, but I saw him look toward the phone every time he turned a page.

At a quarter of nine the phone rang. Lester and I looked at Dad. He got up and went to the phone.

"Hello?" he said. There was a long pause. Too long a pause. "Oh," he said finally. "I'm so sorry."

I closed my eyes and swallowed. Lester didn't move.

"Of course," said Dad. "I can understand how you feel. . . ."

The conversation didn't make sense until I heard him say, "Keep your chin up, Sal."

It wasn't the real estate woman, it was Aunt Sally. And when Dad hung up at last, he said, "Carol's getting divorced."

I stared. "They just got married!" I said.

"Well, a year ago, yes," said Dad.

"When you marry a sailor, you only stay married for a year?" I asked.

"Some things don't work out, Alice, and I guess that elopement was one of them," Dad said. My cousin Carol had left college and gone off to marry a sailor without even telling her parents. "It's a real heartache for Sal and Milt."

"Is she going to go back and live with her folks?" asked Lester.

"No. Sal says she's taken an apartment in Chicago, not too far from them, and that's good, I think. I'm just glad there were no children. A divorce is always hardest on the kids."

I didn't see how a divorce could be worse than a death, though. At least if Mom and Dad were divorced, we could still see them both. I wondered if I should write Carol a sympathy note or something. Maybe I should say that she could always marry a soldier. The evening that had started out exciting—a new adventure—now seemed sad and gloomy. Even if the real estate woman called to tell us we got the house, it wouldn't seem right to be happy. My fifth-grade year was getting worse by the minute.

Nine o'clock became nine thirty and then ten.

"Go on to bed, Al," said Dad. "She won't call this late."

"Rats!" said Lester, and slammed his physics book shut.

I got up from my beanbag chair and had just started for the bathroom when the phone rang again. We all looked at each other as though no one wanted to answer. Finally Dad picked up the phone.

"Yes?" he said. Then "Yes?" again, even louder. I saw his eyes begin to crinkle at the corners and his lips begin to smile. "We *did*?" he cried, and nodded to us.

I'll bet I gave a yell that the real estate woman could hear. Maybe even the Sheaverses could hear it next door. Lester tossed his pen in the air and caught it, and when Dad hung up, we all began yelping like puppies. We all began talking at once. You *can* be sad at one thing and happy about something else both at the same time, I discovered. And at eleven o'clock that evening, on a school night, we were still out in the kitchen, eating ice cream and making plans.

❀ ❀   18   ❀ ❀

Helping Out

I couldn't wait to get to school the next morning to tell the girls. I saw Rosalind and the others in a corner of the playground when I got there. I ran over, eager to tell them my news. But even before I reached them, I could see that Megan was crying and the other girls were trying to comfort her. Dawn had one arm around Megan's shoulder.

"What's wrong?" I asked, looking Megan over to see if she was hurt. I thought maybe she'd fallen off the monkey bars or something.

"It's her sister," said Jody, who then looked at Megan to see if she wanted to tell it. When Megan didn't say anything, Jody said, "Marlene's got a kidney tumor, and she's having an operation."

I tried to imagine a kidney tumor. I didn't even know

where the kidneys were. "I'm really sorry, Megan," I said, and wondered if I sounded sincere.

Megan just cried some more. I put my arm around her too. "When is the operation?" I asked.

"T-Tomorrow," sobbed Megan. I guess you still cry for a sister even when you can't stand her.

"Are you going to be at the hospital?"

She shook her head. "Mom wants me to come to school. She says they'll call me when the operation's over."

"Then we'll stick by you all day tomorrow," I promised, and the other girls nodded their heads. We patted Megan's shoulder and gave her a hug.

I decided I'd wait until lunchtime to tell anyone about our new home. But all through the geography lesson, while Mrs. Swick was talking about Lewis and Clark, I thought about Marlene and her kidney tumor. I wasn't sure what a tumor was, but I knew it wasn't good.

How were you supposed to feel, I wondered, when somebody you didn't like very much got sick? When that person might die? When deep down inside of you, you were sort of, kind of, well . . . not exactly glad, but maybe not too sorry, either?

But that thought seemed so awful, so terrible, I was ashamed to have thought it. Rosalind was probably the only other person I could tell that to, and I was sure she would understand. But when I sat down beside her at lunch, I wondered if maybe it was even too awful to tell Rosalind, so I didn't.

We needed something nice to talk about instead, and because Megan and Jody and Dawn were still in line with their trays, I decided to go ahead and tell Rosalind about the new house.

"Guess what!" I said.

"You got another cat?" she guessed.

"No. I'm never going to get another cat. Something else."

"I don't know."

"Dad bought a house in Silver Spring."

Rosalind stopped chewing and just stared at me. "You're going to move?"

And suddenly I knew that this might be good news to me, but it sure wasn't for Rosalind. Sara, our other best friend, had moved away. Megan was sad over her sister's kidney, and Jody and Dawn weren't exactly our "best" friends. What was there for Rosalind to be happy about?

She snapped another bite off her hamburger and shrugged. "So?" she said, and chewed as though she wasn't even tasting it. "What do I care?"

I stared back at her. It wasn't *my* fault we were moving! I hadn't told Dad to buy a house. It wasn't *my* fault that Sara had moved away. It wasn't *my* fault that Marlene's kidney had a tumor. I hadn't had such a good year either. My cat died, my dad wasn't getting married after all, Lester broke his ankle. . . . Wasn't anybody sorry for *me*?

But as the afternoon went on I kept glancing over at Rosalind during our history lesson and I watched her during math. I caught her looking out the window, her mouth turned down at the corners, and she reminded me of how Lester looked when he thought he couldn't go to the prom.

And even though I could have said something mean back to Rosalind at lunch—told her that if she didn't care, then I didn't either—I remembered that I wanted to be a helper, not a hurter. I wanted to make things better, not worse.

When the last bell rang and Rosalind was putting books in her backpack, I went over and said, "Lester's prom is on Saturday. Do you want to come over and spend the night?"

Rosalind looked up.

"We could take a picture of him in his tuxedo jacket and shorts and watch him drive off in a limousine."

Rosalind began to smile. "Okay," she said. "And eat at your place?"

"Sure," I said. "You can come for dinner, too."

The next day at school we stayed with Megan wherever she went. We crowded around her at recess and sat with her through lunch. It was like we made a wall around her so no other bad news could get through.

About two in the afternoon the secretary's voice came over the loudspeaker. "Mrs. Swick, would you please send Megan Beachy to the office? There's a phone call."

Megan got up from her seat without smiling. I thought maybe her legs wobbled a little bit. Mrs. Swick knew about Megan's sister. She glanced around the room. "Alice, would you go to the office with Megan, please?" she said.

"Yes," I said quickly. I followed Megan out the door.

In the hall I grabbed Megan's hand, and it felt cold. I couldn't think of anything to say, so I just squeezed it. She squeezed back.

When we got to the office, Miss Otis told Megan to go in and see the principal, and I sat down outside to wait. Miss Otis looked over at me and gave me a worried smile. I gave her a worried smile back.

One minute went by. Then two minutes. What if Marlene had died? What if the operation didn't help and they had to remove her kidney? Could you live without a kidney? I wondered if I should be praying while I watched for Megan, but then I wondered why I had to tell God how worried we were. If He was God, didn't He know already?

The door to Mr. Serio's office swung open, and

Megan came out. She was smiling. The principal was smiling. "That's very good news, Megan," he said.

I stood up and Megan came over. "Dad said everything went well, and the doctor says Marlene will be fine," she said, and gave a big sigh, as though all the worried air in her chest was coming out and she was breathing in only happy things.

I hugged her and Miss Otis smiled. We smiled back. And all the way down the hall Megan talked about a funny card she was going to make for Marlene in the hospital. You folded paper and cut it in such a way that when you opened it up, it looked like a bird opening its beak and saying hello.

The thing about being a helper is that when other people are happy, they want to share it with you. When you're a hurter, they don't want you around.

"I have some sparkles you could glue to the card," I said.

"Perfect!" said Megan.

During our afternoon break we took a jump rope and let Megan jump the longest.

"Look!" Dawn said suddenly.

We let the rope dangle and looked toward the steps where Mrs. Swick was talking with another teacher. They were *laughing*. Mrs. Swick was *laughing*. I think it was the first time I had seen the dimples in her cheeks when she laughs. No one even knew she had dimples.

When the bell rang and I stopped at the drinking fountain, I heard one teacher say to the other, "She and Tom are so happy. They've wanted a baby for so long. . . ."

I knew right away they were talking about Mrs. Swick. When I walked in the classroom, I stared at my teacher and listened to the new sound of her laugh. Maybe she had been trying for years and years to have a baby. Maybe her doctor had put an egg and sperm together in a laboratory and she had just heard the news. Maybe they were going to China and adopting a baby there. It didn't matter. Somehow I wanted to show Mrs. Swick how happy I was for her.

That afternoon I got out my colored pens and a sheet of notebook paper. I wrote *Congratulations!* one letter in pink and the next in blue. Pink . . . blue . . . pink . . . blue. . . . Underneath I wrote, *Lovingly Alice*, and then I left it on her desk.

When I got home from school, Lester was eating Fritos at the kitchen table. He didn't have to use crutches anymore and could put weight on the foot that was in the cast. I would think that a person who could walk on his own two feet again would want to be nice to everybody in the whole wide world, but Lester said something mean.

"Al," he told me, "when we get our new phone

number at the other house, I don't want you to give it to Mickey. Understand?"

"What am I supposed to say if she asks?"

Lester shrugged. "I don't know. Tell her anything," he said.

I thought about that while I made myself a piece of cinnamon toast. How could I be a helper, not a hurter, if I lied? I wondered.

19

Lester's Big Night

"There's too much trouble in the world," I told my father when he came home that evening.

Dad had worked late at the Melody Inn, and Lester and I had eaten supper without him. We'd made a casserole of baked chicken and rice and left some in the fridge for Dad.

"What trouble were you thinking about in particular?" he asked, waiting for the microwave to ding.

"Like how if Mickey is happy, then Lester is mad. And if Lester is happy, then Mickey is sad," I said.

"Come again?" said Dad.

"He doesn't want her to have our new phone number."

"Then don't give it to her."

"She'll *ask*, Dad! I know!"

"Then you'll have to learn the fine art of diplomacy," he said.

"What does that mean?"

"Giving people an answer that won't hurt their feelings," he told me.

Wouldn't you know that about eight thirty that same evening Lester was sitting on the couch with his foot propped up on the coffee table when the phone rang. I answered and knew right away it was Mickey.

I turned desperately toward Lester.

Is it Mickey? he mouthed.

I nodded.

Lester leaped up from the couch and went clumping out the front door so I wouldn't have to lie.

"Could I speak to Les?" Mickey asked.

"He's out," I said.

"Would you ask him to call me when he comes back?" Mickey said.

I knew I could promise to tell Lester to call her, but I couldn't promise he would. She must have been thinking the same thing—that he might not call back—because she said, "Oh, never mind him, Alice. I just wondered . . . Well, I have some decisions to make, I guess."

I waited for her to say good-bye, but she didn't.

"The thing is," Mickey went on, "I can't tell if Les is avoiding me or just playing hard to get."

I shaped the words with my mouth but didn't actually say them: *Avoiding you, Mickey. Avoiding you.*

"Can you . . . does he . . . well, does Les ever talk about me at home? I mean, I know he's taking Lisa to the prom; how could he *not,* the way she comes on to him. But I need to know if I have any chance with Les. Just between you and me, does he ever say anything nice about me?"

I was standing with my back against the wall while we talked, and I let my feet slowly slide out from under me until I was sitting on the floor. The one thing they never teach you in fifth grade is the Fine Art of Diplomacy.

"Well, he talks about a lot of people," I said.

The front door opened, and Les stuck his head inside. When he saw that I was still on the phone—sitting on the floor, in fact—his eyes opened wide and he made a cutting motion across his throat, which meant, I guess, that if I didn't hang up soon, I was dead meat. Then he popped back out again.

"But when he mentions my name," Mickey was saying, "is it good, bad, or indifferent?"

"Well," I said, "it's different."

"Different how, Alice? I mean, if I just knew for sure how he felt about me, it would make things a lot easier."

Dad lowered his newspaper and looked at me,

wondering why I was carrying on a conversation with Lester's friend. "I think maybe Dad wants to use the phone," I said quickly.

"Okay. But I wanted to get the phone number to your new house," she said.

"We don't have it yet," I told her.

"Then I'll call again in a few weeks," she said.

When I hung up and Lester came in, I threw back my head and bellowed, "Don't anybody give me our new phone number until after we move, and then I won't have to lie to Mickey."

"Okay by me," said Lester.

Every day that week, though, seemed a little better than the one before. My cat was dead—nothing could change that—but Megan's sister was going to be all right, Mrs. Swick was going to get a baby, we were moving to a bigger house, Lester was going to the prom, and Mickey didn't call back. My fifth-grade year was finally heading in the right direction.

On Saturday, Rosalind came over around four and we sat on the couch drinking lemonade and waiting for Lester to finish dressing for the prom. Dad had come home from the Melody Inn early to help him get ready, and Rosalind and I were in charge of making sure Lester didn't leave without his wallet, the tickets, and the corsage for Lisa.

We could hear the electric razor going in the bathroom.

"Let me see your leg," Rosalind said suddenly.

"Which one?"

"The one Jody said would grow hair like a gorilla because you shaved it and then stopped."

I'd forgotten. Now I couldn't remember which one it had been. I stuck out my left leg. Then my right one. I couldn't tell the difference. "Whew!" I said.

I had a stack of old notebook paper on the coffee table, and we were playing tic-tac-toe while we waited. Rosalind traced the outline of her hand on the back of one of the papers, and I traced my foot on another. Then Rosalind laid her head sideways on a piece of paper, and I tried to trace her forehead and nose and lips, but that didn't work so well.

"Dad!" Lester yelled from the bathroom. "I can't get the stupid collar right."

Dad was smiling as he came out of the kitchen and went down the hall to the bathroom. He was in there for several minutes.

"Stupid penguin suit!" we heard Lester say. Rosalind and I put our hands over our mouths and giggled.

"If we ever go to a prom, let's wear jeans," said Rosalind.

There was the sound of a car pulling up out front, and we scrambled up on our knees to look out the window.

A stretch limousine was parked outside. It was so long that it took up about all the curb space in front of our house. Neighbors came out on their steps to look at it, and Donald Sheavers came running across our yard, trying to see in the windows of the limo.

The driver got out and smiled at Donald. Donald tried to open one of the doors, but the driver shook his head.

We heard Lester clumping down the hall on his cast, and we turned around. There he was in his black tuxedo jacket with his white ruffled shirt and a red bow tie. And instead of tuxedo trousers with a stripe down the side, he was wearing red, white, and blue satin boxer shorts, the stripes in front, the stars on his behind. He had a black sock and a shiny black patent-leather shoe on one foot, his white cast on the other.

Suddenly he stopped. "Oh no!" he said. "I forgot to whitewash my cast!"

"What?" said Dad.

"Look at it!" said Lester. "It's all grimy and dirty. I can't go to the prom looking like that."

"Les, you've got Lisa and two other couples waiting for you to pick them up," Dad said. "There isn't time."

"We'll do it!" I sang out. "Rosalind and I can do it!"

I ran to the hall closet and got out a little bottle of white shoe polish that Aunt Sally had left on her last trip here. I remembered it because she insisted on polishing my sneakers, and I never heard of anybody polishing sneakers before in my life. There was an applicator inside the bottle, and Dad got a sponge from the kitchen. We poured some of the polish in a bowl. I used the applicator, Rosalind used the sponge, and we worked at painting Lester's cast until the whole thing was gleaming white.

The limousine driver came to the door. "Limo service!" he said when Dad opened it.

"He'll be right there," Dad said. He straightened Lester's bow tie and showed him which button to keep buttoned on the jacket. I made sure that Lester had his wallet and the corsage, and Rosalind checked to make sure he had the tickets. Then we all went outside to watch him ride off in the limo.

When the driver went around to get in himself, he found Donald sitting in the driver's seat, and we hooted and laughed when he pulled him out.

"Can't I ride with you as far as the corner?" Donald asked.

"Sorry, dude," the driver said. "It's not on the agenda."

I wondered if that's what I should say to Mickey if she called again and asked for our new phone number. *Sorry, Mickey. It's not on the agenda.*

About an hour later the limo came back again, this time with Lisa and the two other couples. They all came into our house so Dad could take pictures. Lisa was beautiful in a long red dress with no straps at all to hold it up.

"How does a dress like that stay up?" I asked Rosalind.

"Breasts," she said.

Lisa heard and looked around.

"Zipper," she said, pointing to the long zipper down her back. I was embarrassed, but Lisa just laughed.

This time Lester let Rosalind and me go out and peek inside the limo, and I was glad because I could tell Aunt Sally that I had checked, and there wasn't a Jacuzzi in sight.

Rosalind and I ate dinner with Dad. Then we spent the rest of the evening in my room, playing cards on my bed. I was thinking how Rosalind had trusted me enough to tell me that she had started her periods, so I finally got up my nerve and told her a secret in return.

"Rosalind," I said, "have you ever had a thought so evil that you've never told anyone before?"

Rosalind lowered her cards and looked at me. "So awful that if you ever said it aloud, you'd go to hell?" she asked.

I sucked in my breath. "I don't think we believe in hell," I told her.

"I'm not sure I do either, but Megan does, and she

knows a lot more about it than we do," Rosalind said. "If there *is* a hell, is the thought bad enough that you'd go there if you just said it out loud?"

"Probably," I answered.

Rosalind seemed to be thinking it over. "Then write it on a sheet of paper," she said. "But don't sign it."

I tore out a little piece of notebook paper and started to write. I cupped one hand over it so Rosalind couldn't read it until I was done. *I sort of wished that if somebody had to die, it would have been Marlene instead of my cat.* Then I handed the paper to Rosalind.

She studied it for a minute or two and then, without saying a word, crumpled it up and went across the hall to the bathroom where she flushed it down the toilet.

"God can see in sewers," I said.

"The ink's all washed off by now," said Rosalind.

"It's horrible, I know, but I miss my cat," I said.

"As much as you miss Sara?" asked Rosalind.

Now I *knew* I was bad for sure, because I missed Oatmeal even *more* than Sara. I nodded.

"Well, you know what they say," said Rosalind. "When somebody dies, it's because God wanted them in heaven with Him."

I thought about that and began to smile a little. "That means He'd rather have my cat around Him than Marlene Beachy."

"Who wouldn't?" said Rosalind, and she smiled too.

But as I lay awake that night beside Rosalind, who snores, I wondered if my mother died because God had wanted her, too. I wished He'd pick on some other family for a change. But maybe He didn't have anything to do with it in the first place.

Finally I rolled over, away from Rosalind's breath in my face. "Have a good time with Oatmeal," I said to God.

20

Saying Good-bye

When I woke in the morning, I went out in the kitchen before Rosalind was awake to see if Lester had had a good time. Dad was drinking his coffee and working a crossword puzzle.

"Did Lester have a good time?" I asked.

"I don't know," said Dad. "He's not home yet."

I didn't move. "He hasn't come *home*?"

"No. They went from the prom to an all-night pool party, remember? He should be along shortly."

The words were hardly out of his mouth when we heard a car pull up, and someone dropped Lester off. When he came in, he was still wearing his red, white, and blue satin shorts, but he had a T-shirt on top. He carried his tuxedo jacket in one hand and his shoe in the other. He hadn't been in the water, of course, but from the look on his face, he'd had a wonderful time.

"Good morning," Dad said, smiling at him. "How did it go?"

"The best!" said Lester. "Everyone was taking pictures of me in my shorts, Dad. I was like . . . the star! Everywhere we went, people took pictures of Lisa and me. She had a blast!"

"That's great," Dad said. "I'm glad it all worked out. Want some breakfast?"

"No. They served it there."

I wondered when Lester was going to thank *me*, The Girl Who Got Him to Go to the Prom After All. I guess if you're going to be a helper, you have to remember that not everyone says thank you.

"Lisa sure looked pretty," I said.

"Yeah. She was *hot!*" said Lester. "All the guys were hitting on her. And you should see her in a bathing suit! Wow!"

Dad just smiled.

"Was Mickey at the prom?" I asked.

"Yeah. She brought some guy I never saw before. Someone from another school, I think." Suddenly Lester stared at the doorway behind me and said, "What's *that*?"

I turned and saw Rosalind standing there. Her hair was a mess, and one pajama leg was rolled halfway up her thigh. Her eyes were still puffy with sleep, but when Lester said what he did, they popped open. I wondered how she felt just then.

"It's a beautiful princess who just woke up," I said.

"So it is," said Lester. "Good morning, Rosalind."

She came over and sat down in the chair next to me. She reached for a sweet roll and began to eat.

"He had a good time," I said to Rosalind. "He was really cool, and Lisa was really hot."

Lester laughed. "Man, I'm going to bed." He headed for the basement. "Don't anyone wake me unless the house is on fire."

"Happy dreams," I told him.

Lester had a lot of happy things to dream about. Dad had promised him that as soon as he got his cast off, they would go buy a used car. Each day Lester tacked another used-car ad on the bulletin board above the phone: Curtis Chevrolet; Rosenthal Honda; Century Ford. . . . There was even a car dealership called Lester Buick. Lester had circled some of the ads in red and put stars by the cars he especially liked.

But I had something happy to think about too. A new house, new room, new porch, new yard. Life comes in waves, I guess, good and bad, like at the ocean. I'd only been to the ocean once that I could remember—right after we'd moved to Maryland. There were waves that came crashing in and knocked me down, dragged me under for a moment. And there were gentle rocking waves that I could lie on, that rolled me gently to the sand.

On the last day of school Mrs. Swick smiled a lot. She laughed twice. It's hard to remember sometimes that grown-ups aren't just there to take care of us—that they have all sorts of problems of their own.

At recess Megan had good news and bad news. The good news, she said, was that Marlene was well enough to go to Kings Dominion with the family when they went on vacation. The bad news was that she wouldn't be coming back to our school because her parents were going to enroll both Megan and Marlene in a private school in the fall. She would miss us.

It didn't bother me because I wouldn't be here, but it must have been sad for Rosalind. Sara was gone, I was moving away, and Megan would be in another school.

"Maybe somebody really nice will move into our neighborhood," I told her.

"Yeah, right!" she said.

The bell rang, and I grabbed Rosalind's arm as we walked back to the steps. "Life is like the ocean, Rosalind," I said.

"Huh?" said Rosalind.

"It's sort of like you're a bottle tossing about on the waves. Some waves are rough and throw you around, and—"

"Put a cork in it, will you?" said Rosalind, and went on inside.

That night Mickey called again.

"Hi, Alice," she said. "I wondered if you could give me Lester's new phone number now. You promised, remember?"

I didn't think I'd promised that exactly. I looked desperately at Lester for help.

Mickey? he mouthed. I nodded.

But Lester had the number all ready. I stared. He came over and handed me a piece of paper. *Lester's number,* it said.

"Alice?" Mickey was saying. "Are you there?"

"Yes," I said. "Here's Lester's number." I couldn't believe he was really giving it to her. I held the paper out in front of me and started to read it off.

"Just a minute till I get a pencil," said Mickey.

As I waited, my eyes traveled to the car ads on the wall. *Lester's Buick,* read one of the ads, and the phone number was the same one I was giving Mickey. I wheeled around and glared at Lester.

"Ready," Mickey said when she came back.

I couldn't do it. Not even to Mickey. "You know," I

said, "you'll have to get it from Lester. I can't read his writing. Sorry."

When I hung up, Lester said, "What did you do *that* for?"

"The fine art of diplomacy, Lester," I said. "You're in for it now. God can read car ads, you know."

When school was out for the summer and we were packing to move, I did everything I could with Rosalind. I told her to bring over a box and I would give her all the stuff I didn't want anymore—even some of the things I did want. I gave her a little statue of Smokey the Bear, some purple beads, a rubber stamp with a witch on it, a snow globe, a Snickers bar, yellow shoelaces, a package of gum, sunglasses, a five-thousand-piece jigsaw puzzle of the rain forest, and a picture of me in second grade with two teeth missing.

"No matter what," I said to Rosalind, "you're one of my best friends forever."

"Even if we never see each other again?" she asked.

"We *will*, but even if we don't," I said.

Lester got the cast off his foot, and the next day he and Dad bought a used Chevy. It wasn't the sporty model Les had in mind, but it wasn't an ugly car, either. It was silver with blue bucket seats, and Lester was pretty proud of it.

Rosalind came over that evening, and we sat out on

the steps, watching Lester polishing the headlights and trim. We giggled when a bird pooped on his windshield just after he'd washed it. I went in the house and got him some paper towels.

After he'd programmed his favorite stations on the car radio, he drove around the neighborhood with the windows rolled down so everyone could see he owned a car and could hear him coming.

He came back home a few minutes later to get a can of Sprite to put in his beverage holder, and when he went inside, I got this wild idea.

"If Dad asks, tell him I'm out riding around with Lester," I told Rosalind, and before she could answer, I leaped off the steps, raced to the car, crawled through one of the open front windows so Lester wouldn't hear the car door slam, and dived headfirst into the backseat. I scrunched down on the floor only seconds before Lester came back out.

He jumped in the car, turned the radio on full blast, and took off. And right that minute I realized I had no idea where he was going. Maybe he wasn't just going to ride around the neighborhood for a little bit. Maybe he was going to invite all his friends and fill the backseat with girls.

Hey, Lester! one of them would say. *Looks like we've got a stowaway.*

Help! I should have said. *Stop! I didn't mean it!* But

Lester had all of the windows rolled down, and the air rushing through made the car feel like a convertible. Even though I was on the floor, I could feel my hair blowing about my face. I decided to just relax and see what the evening would bring.

Lester began to sing along with the music:

"Let me feeeel your lips,
 Let me feeeel your touch,
 Get me warm, hot baby,
'Cause I love you so much . . ."

Then the drum came in, and Lester sang along with the beat:

"*Buh-buh* bum-bum *buh-buh*
Buh-buh bum-bum *buh-buh* . . ."

I covered my mouth so he couldn't hear me giggle. He went right on singing the second verse:

"If you like my kisses,
If you tingle and spin,
Let me jive you, baby,
Won't you let me come in . . ."

I couldn't help myself. This time when the drum solo

came in again and Lester started to sing, I warbled along with him:

"*Buh-buh* bum-bum *buh-buh*
Buh-buh bum-bum *buh-buh* . . ."

The car braked, and Lester swerved over to the side of the street and stopped.

"Al!" he yelled.

"Oops!" I said.

"What the heck?" He reached around and grabbed at me, getting a fistful of hair.

"Ouch!" I yelped.

"Get up here!" he ordered.

"I just wanted to try out your new car, Lester," I said in my most pitiful voice.

I slid over the front seat and landed beside him. He looked like he was ready to whack me.

"What do you think you're doing?" he growled.

"It was such a nice night, Lester, and I wanted to ride along with you."

"You don't even know where I'm going," he said.

I took a chance. "Do *you*?"

He gave me a long hard stare, and then he started to laugh. "No," he said. "I just wanted to get a feel for the car myself before I asked my friends along."

"Then let me ride with you," I said.

The car started up again as the singer finished the last verse of the song. Even though I can't carry a tune, I joined in with Lester on the drum solo:

"*Buh-buh* bum-bum *buh-buh*
Buh-buh bum-bum *buh-buh* . . ."

When we got back, Rosalind was still waiting for me on the steps.

"Hey, Rosalind," Lester called. "Want a ride home?"

"Sure," she said.

And we serenaded her all the way back to her place.

"The movers are coming on Monday," Dad said at breakfast. "Do you have to work that day, Les, or can you be here?"

"I'll be working," Lester said.

"Then make sure all your things are packed and ready to go," Dad told him.

Lester had already sold his drum set to pay for his gas and car insurance, so that was one less thing to move. I sort of hated to see those drums go. There were too many changes going on, I decided. I was excited about moving and sorry to leave; I wanted to live in our new house, but I was afraid I'd miss the old one. Lester was driving a car and was more grown up, but I didn't want him to be away too much. I began to feel that if I closed my eyes for one minute, everything would have changed again when I opened them.

Dad took the whole weekend off to sort through stuff. You know the worst thing about moving? You keep needing things you already packed. You know the best thing about moving? You get to eat take-out food because all your kitchen stuff is sealed up in boxes.

I wanted to say good-bye to Rosalind in person, so I walked over to her house and rang the doorbell. The shades were down, and I hoped I wasn't waking anyone up. I rang again and then I knocked, but nobody came.

The woman next door came out of her house and saw me. "They're not home," she called. "They've gone to Wisconsin for two weeks."

I stared at her and then at the door. Rosalind hadn't said anything to me about going on a trip. "Are you sure?" I asked.

"Of course. I watched them leave yesterday," the woman said.

I went back home and sat down on a kitchen chair. Dad was packing the last of our cereal into a box along with some bread and crackers.

"Why the long face?" he asked.

"I wanted to tell Rosalind good-bye, and she wasn't home. They've gone on a two-week trip, and I didn't know anything about it," I said.

"Who told you?"

"The woman next door."

"Well," said Dad, "some people aren't very good at good-byes."

I went down the hall to my near-empty room. Maybe I wasn't too good at good-byes either. But I searched around through the boxes piled on my floor till I found the one with my school stuff and papers in it. I was going to write her a note. I picked up one paper and found the outline of Rosalind's hand on it. I studied that hand. I could almost see Rosalind, the way she had sat on the couch tracing it.

I put my own hand over Rosalind's there on the paper. Hers was a little bigger. I took my gold metallic pen and traced my hand just inside of hers. On the palm I wrote, *Best friends forever!*

Suddenly I started to smile. There was a water stain at the bottom of the paper where Rosalind had set her glass of lemonade. I drew a little arrow down to the stain and wrote, *Elephant kiss—from me to you.* I knew that would make her laugh. Then I walked back to Rosalind's house and slid it under the door.